Brighde Restricted

THE AMULET SERIES 3

Brighde Restricted

LESLIE SOMMERS & JANICE SOMMERS

4 Horsemen
Publications, Inc.

4 Horsemen
Publications, Inc.

Published By: 4 Horsemen Publications, Inc.

4 Horsemen Publications, Inc.
PO Box 417
Sylva, NC 28779
4horsemenpublications.com
info@4horsemenpublications.com

Cover & Typesetting by Autumn Skye
Linebreak Image Pendant drawn by Niki Tantillo
Edited by Gayle Staggemeyer

Library of Congress Control Number: 2024939675

Paperback ISBN-13: 979-8-8232-0555-9
Hardcover ISBN-13: 979-8-8232-0556-6
Audiobook ISBN-13: 979-8-8232-0558-0
Ebook ISBN-13: 979-8-8232-0557-3

Dedication

For our readers, new and old,
who kept asking for more.

Acknowledgments

To Kait, for talking me down when imposter syndrome rears its face, for reminding me to blow stuff up or kill someone when I'm not sure what my next steps are, and for being a kindred witchy spirit. To AK, for championing us as we were worried this story wouldn't hold up. To Chelsea, for being unwaveringly real (even if I cry), and to Heidi, I treasure our late-night chats about everything and nothing all at once. To the Thursday Girls, I wouldn't trade any of our get-togethers for anything in this world. To Maggie, thank you for always having our backs when the chips are down. To Dawn, when we struggle to continue with this dream, I remember you asking, "WHAT HAPPENED?!" after reading *Brighde Reborn*, and it encourages us to keep going. To Crystal, for keeping her niece informed about every part of this writing journey and for getting her hooked on the story. To Lin, who had to buy her own copies because her granddaughter wouldn't share. And last but most definitely not least, thank you to our lovely editor, Alexa, who challenges us to challenge ourselves and makes us stronger writers. We are so lucky to have found you and feel so honored you let us come back book after book.

viii Brighde Restricted

Table of Contents

DEDICATION V
ACKNOWLEDGMENTS VII
CHAPTER 1 1
CHAPTER 2 13
CHAPTER 3 26
CHAPTER 4 35
CHAPTER 5 44
CHAPTER 6 56
CHAPTER 7 65
CHAPTER 8 83
CHAPTER 9 94
PRONUNCIATION 104
PRONUNCIATION 105
ABOUT THE AUTHORS 107
BOOK CLUB QUESTIONS 109

Chapter 1

Waiting for Bridget and her friends to get out of her goodbye party had not been on my bingo card for the day. I thought when she'd replied to my text giving me Annabelle's address, things were wrapping up. Guess who couldn't mark off that square on his card?

I sighed, tucking my hand into my pocket and pulling out my phone. We really needed to work on her punctuality.

I loved my cousin; I really did. Besides being a total badass, she also had the biggest heart of anyone I'd ever met. She was the last person to give up on someone, no matter how many times they'd proven to be a complete and utter asshole.

I mean, look at me.

"Good. See you in the morning," I heard Cole say to Bridget.

"About time," I muttered to myself as I adjusted my position on the hood of her car. At least it was a beautiful night out, not like the icy death we'd had after Samhainn. I shivered. I hated the cold.

"Took you long enough to say goodbye," I said to Bridget as she walked to her car.

She huffed. "After graduation, I don't know when I'll be seeing my friends again. Please forgive me."

Oh, she was annoyed with me. She usually was these days.

"Doesn't matter. Just remember, you can't have much contact with them after you leave. The less people who matter to you, the less likely they'll be hurt—"

"I know, I know, when Beira's warriors come after me for the Amulet," she cut in.

I bit my tongue to stop myself from screaming. Devoting a lot of my time to her education and training this past year didn't seem to have made an impact on her. It was as if she didn't even care the world would end.

She pulled the Amulet from under her shirt and showed it off in the moonlight. Thank Brighde we were alone.

"I can't believe you still wear it. What a stupid thing to do." I shook my head.

"What else am I supposed to do? Mom doesn't know that I found it, and I can't risk leaving it in the house. At least this way, I can always protect it," she said with hostility, flaring that annoyance with me yet again.

"But who will protect you?" I retorted. She didn't know about Logan being her Protector yet, so it was a fun tidbit for me to mention. With her being late to everything, it was my responsibility to train her and get her ready for the big show.

Who else could have done it? Trip? I wrinkled my nose at the thought.

"I can protect myself," she said simply. The car locks disengaged as she opened the driver's door. "Need a ride?"

"Sure." I climbed in and buckled the seatbelt. "You know, I won't be in Switzerland with you. I can only protect you here and now."

"You told me you and Logan were going to Switzerland," she reminded me as we pulled away from the curb. "To find Andrew's family."

"Yes, but I can't do that without you. *You're* the Cuardaitheoir. I can search the ends of the universe hunting down the Amulet, but ultimately, it will only respond to you." I paused. "Don't you feel it?"

She didn't answer me, but I could see her frown, which she displayed when lost in deep thought. I sighed, tired of this conversation already, but she needed to feel more confident in herself.

"Bridget, I know you're scared about the next step of training, but I promise you, the trainer you get will be the best. Our family doesn't do second-string," I said, drawing her attention back to me. "Well, most of the time."

She groaned, but I grinned. A little teasing never hurt anyone.

"Are you ever going to let my dating history go?" She turned toward the high school, getting closer to my house. "I don't even miss him anymore."

I adjusted my shorts that were riding up. "Don't you? You think you're so sneaky, but I know you've been obsessing over your emails to see if he's messaged you."

"I'm completely over him."

"Are you really?" I asked as she pulled into my driveway. "Because we can't let anything distract you from this mission. It's the single most important event of your life."

"Why bother graduating then?" Bridget snapped.

I knew I got on her nerves, but I had to do what I had to do.

I looked at her directly. "Listen, Bridget, I know Logan and I have been driving you insane. And I know Trip meant the world to you, but I have to know you're completely focused on your job. If you aren't... well, it could mean your death."

She hated it when I brought up her mortality.

"I'll be fine," she finally responded.

I opened my door and got out.

"Are you sure?" I asked.

"Yes," she said decisively. "I'll see you tomorrow."

"Goodnight," I said, closing the door. If she didn't want to hear any more about it, I couldn't make her listen.

"Got everything?" my dad asked as we were getting ready to leave for school. He picked up his keys and tucked them into his pocket. Alec was sitting lazily on the couch, scrolling through his phone. He was home on summer break and was enjoying every moment of it.

"Yeah, we're good," I answered for both Logan and me.

Logan looked in the mirror and straightened the collar on his white polo shirt. Why did we have to dress up? We'd be wearing gowns anyway.

Alec glanced up at us and gave me a goofy grin. "Look at my little brother, all grown up."

"Shut up," I said jokingly. "You're coming, right?"

"I'll be there," he confirmed.

Graduation day was here, a high school experience I was fine skipping out on. After moving from school to school, I'd learned to disassociate pretty quickly, and I would be using that skill today. But I knew my dad would be happy to see us walk. My sneakers rubbed the back of my foot as I was heading down the stairs. *Great, a blister.* I didn't bother checking as I broke out into the sunshine. Logan followed me, and we began the four-block walk to the school.

"We'll see you there!" Dad yelled at us from the balcony. I waved goodbye and kept going. I wanted to get this day over with.

We arrived at the gym with students milling about, and I saw Hilary standing with her group of friends. I was spotted by Casey Millington, who nodded in my direction and whispered something to her twin sister Amber.

"I'll see you after," Logan said, clapping me on the shoulder and leaving me alone.

"Yeah," I answered as Hilary turned around and waved at me. I waved back.

I was torn about whether to go over or not. Things had changed in the past four months—we weren't as close as we once were, leaving our conversations limited to what we'd found on each other's social media. Mostly memes.

"Okay, seniors, line up! We're walking down in three minutes!" Principal Sharpe announced through the gym. The decision was made for me. My classmates and I settled into our lines, organizing ourselves by the predetermined height chart, and turned to face the gym doors. I looked around but didn't see anything or anyone fishy. Today would be the perfect day for an attack. It's what I would have done.

"Pomp and Circumstance" was pumped over the loudspeakers, and we shuffled to the bleachers on the football field. Those of us in the front paused, waiting for the rest of the class to reach their seats before we could move forward.

"Thank you, parents and teachers, for joining us in celebrating the graduating class of Ocean City High School!" Mrs. Sharpe began. "Please stand and join us in the national anthem, sung by Leah Young, next year's senior class president!"

Leah Young was talented, but my focus was split. I noticed Bridget shifting in her spot, and I wondered what she was looking at. Immediately, I scanned the crowd to look for any trouble. Logan, who was two rows below me, caught my eye and shook his head. He didn't see anything, either.

Leah finished singing, and everyone sat with muffled echoes of cloth hitting the metal benches. We'd just begun the ceremony, and I was already bored.

As graduation droned on, I tried to pay attention, but the speeches were dull. Who cared how the teachers felt about us? It wouldn't matter much if we couldn't find the second Amulet piece before Trip did.

I bounced my leg impatiently as time dragged on, absent-mindedly letting my shoe grind against my heel. The burgeoning blister from before popped, and liquid seeped into my sock. My right heel was rubbed painfully raw. Pushing my foot forward in the shoe, I felt the skin peel away from the fabric, and I just *knew* it was bleeding. I tugged on the collar of the graduation gown. It was hot out, and sweat was pooling under my arms. Apparently, antiperspirant was just a suggestion.

When I thought I would lose my mind, Mrs. Sharpe stepped in and motioned for the first row of students to stand.

"Ruby Cadence Alexanderia," she called out. Students around me started to move, getting ready for the big moment. It was like the entire senior class had all fallen asleep and woken up at the same time. Things were moving faster now, and my row stood. We proceeded down to the grass and waited as the principal called our names.

"Allison Marie Bonnaro!" I watched as she walked across the field and shook hands with the staff. My classmates shuffled forward as the next kid was called.

"Justin Scott Smith!"

I felt a tap on my shoulder and turned face-to-face with Hilary. She wasn't behind me before, so I could only imagine she'd switched places with someone.

"Hey," she said. "Congratulations. We made it!"

I smiled back at her. "Looks like it."

The line moved up.

"Meet me after for a picture?" she asked.

"Sure." Hilary grinned and melted back into her original spot in our line.

"Bridget Gwendolyn MacNamara!"

I cheered for her along with her other friends and family. I grinned, happy and proud of how far she'd come this past year, despite all the shit I'd given her.

Out of the corner of my eye, I saw Logan at attention. The rest of the kids were looking proud and excited about holding their diplomas, but my friend ignored everyone else and whipped around to look behind me.

Then I smelled it too—smoke.

A scream rang out, and someone shouted, "Fire!"

Bridget!

Chaos exploded as grass was ignited, like someone had turned on a fireplace. I pushed past the crowd and ran to Bridget; she hadn't moved past the podium since receiving her diploma.

Bridget!" I yelled as I found her. Frozen in panic, she looked at me.

"Do something!" I screamed again, finally reaching her. I grabbed her arm and pointed behind Dan Zachariah, who had presumably been tackled onto the grass to put out the flames on his gown.

"Behind him," I told her.

Fire had spread everywhere. Banners behind the bleachers were ignited, sparks feeding the dried-out grass into the inferno, and the mini water bottles that had been passed out did nothing to stop the flames. People were bolting in every direction, making it difficult to put anything out. Smoke billowed, and I heard alarms in the distance.

Bridget looked at me, then closed her eyes. In a moment, we went from the fire's blistering heat to darkness and cool relief as Bridget rained showers on us. It was a start, but it wasn't enough. She needed to do more.

"Come on, Bridget! You can do this!" I yelled over the din. My cousin seemed to pull harder on her powers as the rain intensified, and thick, heavy slushes of ice landed around us. Sleet.

Ignoring it, I paid strict attention to Bridget. She needed me now more than ever.

"Focus," I demanded as she blinked at the scene around her. I got her patented glare, but she did what I asked. I had no idea what she'd tapped into, but she was able to distribute the droplets evenly enough, bringing the fire to submission.

I breathed a sigh of relief as pride flourished within me. I *knew* she could do it!

As the fire died down, the field was left in devastation. Smoky, wet ashes of what used to be grass left patches all over the 50-yard line. The banner was burned to smithereens, and what was left was a soggy, pulpy mess.

"Cay!" I heard Logan calling for me. I spun around and saw him pointing at our enemy.

Trip.

I felt safer leaving Bridget after she'd put out the fire, so I took off to get Trip to myself. The blond asshat stood just beyond the trees; he was watching her and nothing else. My blood sang in my veins, and I had never wished for Alec's powers more in my life.

"Didn't want to miss all the fun?" I asked as I slowed to a saunter.

Trip sneered, focusing his attention on me. "I'm only here for one thing."

"Just one? Here I thought you actually cared about my cousin." I heard Logan behind me. We needed to keep Trip away from Bridget at all costs.

Trip smirked and adjusted his stance. "I've never stopped caring, despite what you think of me."

"This old song and dance? We know, Trip. All you care about is the Amulet."

Trip looked away and sighed before taking a step toward me. "If that's what you want to think. Bridget knows how much I care about her."

I stepped toward him, not backing down from his idle threat.

"I don't think you know how to care. Because if you did, you wouldn't have ghosted her. Or let her think you didn't care about her. Or let her believe she was nothing more than a means to an end." I curled my fingers into a fist at my side, preparing for what was about to happen.

Trip gulped but waved a hand in my face. "I didn't have a choice on ghosting her. That was my parents' doing. I never told her I didn't care, and *you* told her she was a means to an end for me. I'm not the bad guy here. You're more toxic for her than I am."

Heat radiated up my body, and I launched myself at him. I didn't care how it would look or what would happen to me. I only cared about beating him into the mud.

I tackled Trip to the ground and slammed his head on the dirt. He fought back, throwing his fist up to connect with my left shoulder. It hurt, but I shook it off, pulling my arm back to punch him in the face. Blood poured from his nose, and I debated about healing it so I could break it again. Trip cold-cocked the back of my skull with something, and I flinched, grabbing my head as I slipped off him. Logan hauled me up onto my feet and turned to face Trip, always having my back. Trip would be no match for Logan—he was Bridget's Protector and had been training for this most of his life.

I stumbled away from the fray, trying to get my head to stop spinning and ears to stop ringing.

Grunts behind me indicated more fighting was happening, and I turned around to get a glimpse.

Logan and Trip were each throwing a fist or a jab before ducking or landing blows. It was awesome watching Logan do what he did best: kick ass. I took the time to heal my injuries and stop the annoying ringing. Looking around, I put my hand over my eyes like a visor and saw the field was empty except for some camera crews and firefighters lingering for interviews. Bridget was gone, along with the rest of the school.

"Logan," I said. "Wrap it up."

Logan threw one last punch and knocked Trip to the ground. The wind must have been knocked out of him because he was coughing up a lung. Logan just turned and walked away.

"She left?" he whispered.

I nodded and clapped my hands together.

"Well, Trip, as always, this has been ... terrible, and you suck. Ta-ta!" I blew him a kiss, waved goodbye, then went to leave.

Trip was up on his feet, the resilient little jackass. "This isn't over, McKay."

"DM me the details," I called back, walking backward away from him. Logan snickered next to me.

"Next time, I won't go easy on you!"

I flipped him the peace sign and walked toward the school, leaving Trip in the bushes alone.

"**Y**o," Logan said as he nudged my shoe. We were on our way to the airport in the back of an Uber. Alec had a summer job interview he was prepping for, and my dad had a meeting at work he couldn't miss. He knew how important this was to the world and understood my need to get to Bridget to find the pieces.

"What?" It was seven a.m. on summer break, and I was tucked up against the car window in an attempt to catch up on some sleep before we headed through security.

Logan seemed like he didn't want to be the only one awake besides the driver. "We're here, Sleeping Beauty."

I looked out the window and saw the airport looming above us. Its dirty walls and crowded parking lots felt like home to me since I'd spent so much of my life flying and moving. I stretched in the seat as the driver pulled into the drop-off lane. Busy as it was, he slipped into a spot easily, and we hopped out with our bags to avoid his being chased out by the police.

"Thanks! Have a good day, man!" I said, closing the door.

He waved goodbye and put his blinker on to leave the insanity as Logan and I trudged in toward security. We had checked ourselves in already and only had carry-ons. Skipping to the security line, we were stuck waiting as it seemed everyone and their mother were flying out today.

"Shoes off. Jackets, sweatshirts, and hoodies off. Nothing in your pockets. Phones, laptops, tablets, and iPads all go in their own bin," the guards yelled as people milled toward their screenings like the slow drip of molasses. "Did you see that?" Logan asked, nodding his head toward the guards. "They're body-scanning everyone."

"That's weird." I adjusted my backpack strap on my shoulder. We breezed through the passport check to get stuck on the turtle train of the scanners. After dumping our packs in their respective bins, we stripped off our sweatshirts and sneakers and waited in line to be scanned.

"Keep it moving, people. Shoes off!" a guard yelled. Logan and I were quiet as our turn came up for the body scan. He went, was deemed clear, then was pulled out of line for another scan. I was up next.

"Stand on the yellow feet markers. Keep your hands above your head. Don't move," the guard instructed me. I followed the directions and let the giant scan highlight me.

"Step out, please," one guard said. "Stop there."

I stepped, then paused. They scanned me again and waved me on. Logan had already grabbed his stuff and was waiting for me on the side. I snagged my hoodie, bag, and sneakers and trotted over to meet him.

"Strange but not bad," I said.

He nodded. "I wonder what amped it up," Logan said, standing and shaking his foot. He was full of energy, either from anxiety or the energy drink he'd downed before we left. I didn't know which.

"Who knows, but I should check in with Bridget." I slid my phone from my pocket and unlocked it.

[Cay: Are you still wearing it?]

I was hoping she knew I meant the Amulet. I assumed she did, but I didn't want to take any chances.

My phone buzzed in my hand.

[Bridget: Of course. I never take it off.]

I breathed a sigh of relief as we found our gate and sat in two empty seats away from the crowd as much as possible.

"She has it," I said to Logan in a low tone.

"Good," he replied. Logan had become less chatty in the days since we'd been training Bridget. He was more focused on her and his job than ever before. I'd had an inkling he'd caught feelings for her, but I didn't want to call him on it if I was wrong.

"I should warn her about what's been going on."

"That's a good idea. I'm going to grab something to eat. You want anything?" Logan offered as he stood up.

"Whatever you get is fine, thanks." He headed toward the food stall across from our gate, leaving his backpack on the seat.

[Cay: Be careful going through airport security. L & I are here now, and things are tense. Can't risk exposure.]

[Bridget: Tense? What do you mean tense?]

I shook my head. Here I'd thought tense only had one meaning.

[Cay: Just watch your back. Who knows who's a BD.]

Beira's descendant. We really needed to come up with a catchier name for them, but it wasn't high on the list of priorities.

[Bridget: Aren't they always lurking in the shadows?]

I sighed and put my phone back to sleep. She'd been fighting me when I was trying to help, so I needed a break. I leaned back against my seat and slouched, attempting to get comfortable. People wandered aimlessly as they looked around for their gates. Garbled announcements, calling for passengers or announcing flights boarding, were made on the speakers. The smell of hand sanitizer was strong as the dispenser was less than two feet away from my post. The hard back on the seat made it difficult for me to relax, so I sat up, waiting for Logan to return.

"That line was insane," he said, handing me a foil-wrapped hot thing and a coffee. I could smell the bitter brew from here.

"Why?" I unwrapped the foil to reveal a sausage, egg, and cheese bagel sandwich, piping hot. Logan plopped next to me in his chair and opened his own sandwich.

"One cashier, a thousand people," he said before taking a large bite. I followed suit, and we sat there, chewing silently until we'd finished.

The sandwich was as good as I could expect in an airport—a little flavorless, and without the sausage, it would have been bland as hell. What was American cheese even bringing to the table?

Either way, it was filling, and that was all I'd wanted. I crumpled up my garbage, allowing my stomach to wake up and do its job.

"I really hoped once I was done with school, I would have at least one day to sleep in," I complained, taking a sip of my scalding coffee. It was better than the sandwich, but it wouldn't win any awards.

"I gave up sleeping in when I moved in with you," Logan replied.

I feigned insult. "*Moi*? However so?"

Logan smiled as he gave me side-eye. "You roll around in your sleep. I was a room away, but if I didn't know any better, I'd believe you slept with a black bear."

I burst out laughing. "I've always moved in my sleep, but I sound like a bear? Specifically, a black one?"

"Waking up from hibernation. Disoriented and confused."

"I don't think that's specific to black bears." We both laughed, drawing attention from other passengers.

"Do you know how you sleep?" I asked him, taking a breath.

"I know how I sleep!" he said, grinning.

"Oh, please, you're unconscious. How would you know you snore unless someone tells you?"

"I've had no complaints." He took a sip of his black coffee and settled back into his seat.

I adjusted in my seat again. "Consider this a complaint. I'm not sleeping next to you in a hotel room if you snore."

He chuckled and shook his head. "Finish your coffee. Our boarding time is coming up."

"Yeah, yeah. You know I'm right," I joked, taking another swig of the brew. We sat quietly for the rest of the time. Airports were all about hurrying up to wait.

My dad had suggested we not start in Switzerland or Scotland or any place that could lead the Findlays to our plans. We flew into Cardiff first, hoping to throw off any of Beira's people following us. We weren't sure if they were, but we couldn't be too careful. Plus, we were hoping to find more info on the location of Andrew's family before we made it to Switzerland.

Leaving the airport for the night felt very high-risk, and I'd never been happier to have a Protector with me. We hitched a taxi to take us to a hostel in town to crash for the night.

"Fancy a pint?" Logan whispered as we pulled up to our accommodations.

I frowned and leaned over him to see the sidewalk jammed with people, probably tourists shopping. The hostel was in front of us, displaying a light-blue door with yellow trim. The door was wide open and inviting anyone inside, but the camera above the door indicated otherwise.

There was a small bar next to the blue door with tables set out on the patio. The windows behind it were open, allowing us to peek at the wall of liquor behind the bar.

"I'm not really a drinker, but this may be a 'When in Rome' situation..."

Logan shrugged one shoulder. "Up to you. But it would be a shame to not have a drink before we really get to work."

Climbing out of the car, I glanced at the bottles again before looking at my friend.

"Yeah, why not? I don't know if I can focus on any tourist shit right now."

Logan smiled and nodded. "Let's check in, and then we can grab that beer."

We crossed through the blue-and-yellow threshold and were immediately hit with a kaleidoscope of hipster colors: pinks, yellows, and browns decorated with fairy lights. It was overwhelming and kitschy at the same time.

With his bag slung over his shoulder, Logan waited in line at the front desk. He seemed completely unaffected by the dizzying decorations. Streamers hung from the ceiling as if celebrating their tacky décor. I closed my eyes before it got worse.

"Hi, I'm Logan Carter. I have a room booked," I heard my friend say to the hostel worker. Opening my eyes, I noticed she was short and had black, chin-length hair, and she was batting her eyes at Logan. He once again seemed to be completely unaffected. After typing something into the computer in front of her, she handed him a set of keys and pointed us to the stairs.

"Your room is at the top of the hallway, and you can grab the remaining two beds that are open in the room. All rooms have their own private shower and toilet for the roommates to share."

"Thanks," he said, taking the keys and shifting away from the desk. Without looking back, we headed up the stairs and unlocked our door. Inside was a bright room with stark white walls and what I'd call "enthusiastic blue" lining the window trim. The open beds were bunks pressed against the window. I sighed, wondering if I'd be waking up with the sun tomorrow when our flight wasn't until mid-afternoon. I know from experience a trip like this one would require all the sleep we could get.

I dumped my stuff on the top bunk and stepped back for Logan to do the same. He tucked the room keys into his pocket and faced me.

"You good?" he asked.

"Yup. Let's go."

Heading back downstairs, we walked into the bar next door. I was a little nervous, waiting for someone to come kick us out for being underage, like it was stamped on my forehead or something. Logan looked cool as could be, like he'd done this a million times before.

He definitely hadn't.

We grabbed seats at the bar since the place was kind of empty. It was about eleven in the morning, so I guessed people in Europe didn't drink on weekdays before the afternoon. Logan picked up a menu from a few seats away and reviewed it before sliding it over to me.

My high school reputation was that of a bad boy, but in reality, I didn't drink. The beer my friends often had tasted watery and cheap, and I never really enjoyed the dizziness I got.

"Need help?" The bartender came over to place two small napkins in front of us before resting her hands on the bar.

"I'll have cider," Logan said smoothly.

She nodded and looked at me expectantly.

"Um…" I looked at the menu again, a rush of panic creeping up my neck.

"He'll have the same," Logan cut in. She nodded again and walked off to get us the drinks.

"Thanks," I said sheepishly.

It was only with Logan that I could let my guard down. He was my best friend, and we'd been through so much together. He was Bridget's Protector, and I couldn't have been happier it was him and not some douche like Tomas.

"No problem. It's basically sparkling apple cider."

I sighed, feeling the jet lag kick in. There was something in the back of my brain that kept pinging, like a forgotten reminder, but I couldn't remember what.

The bartender came back with our drinks and promptly left us as another person sat down at the other end of the bar.

We each picked up our overflowing glasses as Logan raised his. "Cheers," he said, gently tapping his pint against mine, causing the golden alcohol to spill over the lip of each glass. It poured over my fingers, leaving a sticky trail in its wake.

"Sorry."

"Nah, man. All good." I sipped my cider, mild bubbles fizzing on my tongue. The crisp apple flavor flooded my taste buds, but with a slightly sour aftertaste. I took another sip before deciding it tasted great.

"So, tell me," I said, licking my lips and placing the pint back onto the napkin, "when did you start drinking?"

Logan grinned. "Back in my training days. After a long day of training, one of the older recruits would sneak beer in for us. I didn't love the taste of the beer, but once, they brought in cider. Since then, it's been my go-to."

"I can see why." I took another sip. "This is delicious."

He smirked and took a long drink from his cider.

"I feel like we haven't caught up in a while." I played with the napkin my cider rested on. Idle hands, and all that. "All this shit with the Amulet has taken over, and we haven't been just Cay and Logan for a bit."

Nodding, Logan put his pint down. "Then I guess it's good we have right now to talk."

"I guess so." I took my own long drink, and I slowly began to feel lighter than I had in a while. The tension I'd felt was slipping away.

"Have you heard from anyone since you graduated?" Logan asked.

"My phone's blowing up with notifications of how often I've been tagged. And it's been, like ... every four hours."

He chuckled at me and downed the rest of his drink. I looked at my own half-full glass and tried to chug it. I choked and coughed, dribbling cider down my chin.

"Shit." I grabbed a napkin and dabbed my face, looking around to see if only Logan had caught my audition for the Beer Olympics. Thankfully, the restaurant was filled with people who were too involved in their own conversations to worry about me.

Logan was laughing and handed me another napkin for my shirt. "Smooth."

"Yeah, yeah." I swirled the remaining liquid in the glass and downed it. That time was better. "There isn't anyone here I'm trying to impress."

"Another one?" The bartender popped up out of nowhere to stand in front of us. Logan glanced over at me with an eyebrow raised.

"Sure." I slid my empty glass in her direction.

"And two glasses of water," Logan added.

"Still or sparkling?"

"Still."

She tapped her finger on the bar twice and flitted off, leaving our empty pints in front of us.

"Is there anyone you're trying to impress these days?" Logan asked as we waited for our drinks.

"Not really. I don't know. It feels like all we've talked about lately is the Amulet, and Bridget, and that asshole." I crumpled my napkin in my fist.

Logan nodded. "Yeah. But the world might end, so it makes sense. Not a lot of space to think about much else."

"True."

The mood turned somber, and I wasn't in the mood for hashing out heavy shit. The bartender brought over the drinks.

"Do you want anything to eat?" she asked.

Logan and I looked at each other.

"Probably," I said, nodding at her. "Can we see a menu?"

Without a word, she turned around and snatched two laminated papers from behind her, placing them in front of us.

"Just let me know what you want," she said before walking off to another patron, again leaving the empty glasses.

I looked over the menu and saw a lot of stuff I knew I wouldn't eat and then spotted chicken fingers. I sat back, knowing my order.

"You good?" I asked Logan. He nodded and flagged the bartender. She came over after a minute.

"What can I get for you?"

"I'll have the chicken fingers," I said.

"And I'll have the mac and cheese," Logan added.

"Anything else?"

We shook our heads.

"I'll be back with your food shortly." And she was off again.

"Where were we?" I asked, picking up my pint and taking a healthy mouthful.

"Talking about the Amulet and the end of the world. And people we may or may not want to impress." Logan took a sip of water and then picked up his cider.

"Oh, that. Well, I've already told you there isn't anyone on my radar these days. What about you?"

I kept drinking my cider, the crisp flavor distracting me from the task at hand. Logan cleared his throat, drawing my complete attention.

Perking up, I shifted in my seat. "I'll take your silence to mean there *is* someone you want to impress."

Logan squirmed and looked away, which was a tell he was hiding something. He'd been doing it since we were ten. When we'd play a card game called "Bullshit," which was based on lying, he'd always shift away from me and avert his eyes, and I'd call his bluff every time. I felt like letting him off easy and not prolonging the torture, for once in his life.

Grinning, I said, "I get three guesses, and the first two don't count."

Chapter

3

"Fine."

Logan took a sip of his water, and the food arrived moments later. Once it was set, he took a large bite of his mac and cheese.

"Bridget," I said, taking a bite of my chicken finger. The food reminded me of home and was worth a moment of silence as we chewed.

"What about her?"

I sighed and wiped my fingers on the napkin. "I know you like her."

"How do you know?" Logan sat back.

I smiled. "From the way you looked at her during all our trainings. You think I didn't notice you cheering her up when she was stuck in her head?"

Logan scoffed. "You were being terrible to her. She needed the pick-me-up."

"I wasn't any worse than what you probably went through," I jokingly grumbled, eating a fry.

"But she wasn't used to it."

"You're missing the point, bro. I know you like her, regardless of how you view my coaching style." He didn't say anything. "I firmly believe in Bridget, but I can't help but worry," I added.

Logan nudged me with his leg. "That's why I'm here."

"I know. But she's my cousin. And my best friend."

He sighed and took another bite of mac and cheese. I sat back and raised my eyebrows at him. There was time to talk about this and a many other splendid things later. Preferably a time that wasn't focused on our potential impending deaths.

"Do you remember us playing cards when we were kids?" I asked.

"Of course."

"Remember how I always knew you were lying?"

"Yeah."

"I know you're lying. Or, at least, avoiding the truth."

Logan picked up his cider and sat back into the chair again as I leaned forward to grab a piece of chicken. After dunking it in some kind of chili sauce, I ripped into the meat and chewed it, waiting for him to make a move.

"Okay, fine, I like her. But that doesn't matter."

"And why not? I say go for it. You're a much better choice than her ex." I wiped my fingers on the extra napkin and picked up my own cider. I took another mouthful, the bubbles bursting against my tongue. It was such a pleasant sensation.

"Cay, I'm her..." he said, looking around before dropping his voice, "Protector. It's probably against the rules."

I knew Logan got too into his head sometimes, but this was the first time I recognized the job weighing on him. His shoulders were slouched as he slumped in his seat, and he idly tapped the side of his pint glass while staring at the liquid inside.

Trying to lighten the mood, I scoffed and took another drink. "Whose rules? Where are these rules? Can I see them?" I wiggled my fingers at his pocket in jest.

"Stop it." Logan nudged me with his foot again. "You know what I mean. I'm supposed to protect her, not date her."

"Why not do both? Because if you keep brooding, I may have to smack you over the head with something heavy. Though, as much as I support you two getting together, I don't want more details than 'date her' while I'm eating. Anyway, I'm fairly confident the only person who would stop you from dating her is Bridget herself." I tapped a finger against my chin. "Though, she did date Trip, and he's the biggest loser out there, so she may not know any better."

Logan flipped me off, and I laughed before finishing my cider. I noticed he was still a half a pint behind me, and I felt some kind of pride.

"But seriously, my friend," I said, grinning, "I think she's ready for a good guy like you. I wholeheartedly support this relationship, if it does happen."

Look at that. I was more like my cousin than I'd realized. I, too, was a sentimental fool.

Logan took another bite of his meal and rubbed the back of his neck. "Thanks, man. It really means a lot to hear you say that."

We spent the rest of the day chatting and drinking before dragging our slobbering, messy selves up to our room and passing out until morning. We then checked out of the hostel and stumbled onto the train, newly purchased sunglasses covering our eyes, and let it take us to the airport.

Once we were off the plane, away from the safety of the airport, we headed toward the bus depot on the other side of Dublin. We'd be spending our day at Trinity College in order to find more information on Beira, Brighde, and the Amulet. Nothing like a good research session to wake up the senses.

"Do you think we'll find anything?" Logan asked as we climbed onto the bus. It was a blue-and-yellow double-decker, popular in the main part of Dublin from what my research told me. We handed over our fare and clambered into the back seats on the first level.

"I hope so. We need to find it more than ever," I replied. "The nightmare at graduation? Sleet in summer!"

Logan nodded. "You trained her well enough, Cay. Have faith in her."

I scoffed. "I have nothing but faith in her. I know she's going to save us all."

Logan patted my shoulder, and we fell back into comfortable silence as the bus left the airport lot.

It was just past lunchtime when we made it to the college. Tourists rushed past us as they were trying to find the library. We wanted the library, too, but not the one with the *Book of Kells*, the one which required tickets for entry. Logan and I wandered around and found one of the libraries, but he stopped before we made it to the door.

"What's up?" I asked.

He pointed to a broken golden ball that sat outside. It brought back memories of a puzzle I'd done when I was a kid. The pieces had been intertwined with each other and formed a sphere when the puzzle was finished. This puzzle looked like it was missing a few pieces.

"It's the *Sfera con Sfera*," Logan told me, looking at his phone. "A sphere within a sphere."

He circled the sculpture, looking at it from all angles until I cleared my throat.

"This is a really cool piece of art, but we're on a deadline," I reminded him.

"We can take some time to admire the hard work of Arnaldo Pomodoro," he replied. Pulling up his phone again, he continued. "It's one of many sculptures with the same name, all of them depicting a different map of destruction."

"Where are the other ones?" I hiked my bag up onto my shoulder and waited for him to answer. Logan loved to learn. When he was in training, we'd keep in touch like pen pals, and he would always focus heavily on what he'd been taught that week. Over time, it dawned on me that being a Protector was his job, but learning was his life.

"All over the world. At least two in Rome, one in Tel Aviv... Oh! There's one at Princeton University." He looked up at me. "We should go see it when we get back."

After this whole nightmare is over.

"Deal," I promised. "Ready to head in?"

"Right. Lead the way." He gestured for me to head inside, and I did, fully expecting him to follow me.

A hush fell over us as we walked in, and the silence was almost punishing. A tall, brutish figure marked the entranceway, reminding me of something I'd built playing Minecraft: harsh blocks forming stoic-looking balconies. We quickly headed to the help desk and used the public computer. Locating any books with references to the Amulet was our first step in trying to help Bridget. I looked at my phone. She would be arriving at the Zurich airport now, if she wasn't on the ground already.

Logan grabbed a pencil and paper and scribbled something.

"I found some books," he said, returning the pencil to its stand. "We need to find the reference section first."

I turned in a circle, feeling a little dizzy. Jet lag must have been kicking in. "Where do we start?"

"Not sure." Logan located a librarian and quietly asked him something. I assumed it was about the reference section, and after a minute, he trotted back.

"It's up two floors and in the back," he said. We wasted no time getting up those stairs and to the stacks. I breathed in their earthy paper and smiled. I couldn't explain it—I really loved research.

Logan searched the stacks while I grabbed an empty table. Since school was out, it was pretty quiet, even for a library. People didn't need as many reference books over the summer, it seemed.

He came back and dumped five books onto the table.

"This was all they had based on our search." Nothing outwardly seemed like it would contain any information we needed, but I picked up a book about the Celtic gods and perused, skimming the pages to find anything referencing Brighde, the Amulet, Switzerland, or Beira.

"This has nothing," Logan said, closing a book he was reading and pushing it to the side. "It mentioned Brighde as St. Brigid, so not what we want or need."

He grabbed another and opened it. We found mentions of Brighde and Beira, but none of the Amulet. There was some information about Switzerland, but nothing was remotely helpful on the location of Andrew's descendants. I appreciated a good research session, but even this was getting me down.

"This one tells me what powers the sisters have but nothing about the Amulet." I sighed and added it to Logan's discard pile. "Should we just start in Switzerland?"

"This one may have something," Logan whispered, despite our being the only ones on the floor. "It says both sisters have ruins in Scotland and that Beira's throne was said to be in Ben Nevis. It's a huge mountain range in Inverness."

"That sounds like the best place to start. I'm not finding any important references or notes on Switzerland or Andrew's family," I answered, closing another book. I took out my phone and noticed that we were way past lunch, and my stomach grumbled. Standing, I stretched and groaned. "Why don't we get some grub, get some rest, and then figure out if we need to head to Scotland or Switzerland? My research from home did say to start there for his family."

"Sounds good to me." Logan took a picture of the pages, closed the book, and returned it all to the restocking cart.

"You're such a Boy Scout," I teased.

He shrugged and smiled at me. "A leopard can't change its spots."

"I'm not trying to change your spots," I said. "I'm merely calling them out."

We left the library and headed toward the street. The sun was beginning its slow descent into darkness, but we had plenty of time left. It didn't set until nearly ten o'clock during Irish summers.

Every shop or restaurant we passed smelled so good, and it was getting hard to pick what I wanted to eat.

"What smells like the best meal in the world to you?" I asked Logan as we passed a fish and chip shop.

"Everything smells like the best meal right now," he said, patting his stomach.

"I know. How about here?" I pointed to a burger joint that looked delicious and uncomplicated.

"Sure." We went in and saw that the menu was smaller than a business card.

"So... it's just burgers and fries," I said.

"According to their sign, it's a delicacy here in the UK." Logan pointed at the sign above us.

"Burgers and fries?" I replied dubiously.

"Yup."

"Okay, sounds good. I'm too hungry to go on," I whined, wrapping my arms around my stomach.

"Same," Logan agreed.

We each ordered a cheeseburger with fries and a milkshake—chocolate for me, strawberry for Logan.

Not wanting to delay eating any longer, we dug in and devoured our meals.

"That was the best idea we've had all day," Logan said, wiping his mouth with a napkin.

"Yeah, considering how our research went."

We took a hop-on, hop-off bus in the center of the town, and it dropped us off a couple blocks away from our hotel. As we settled into our room, I let Logan use the bathroom first while I looked up more about whether we should go to Scotland or Switzerland next.

"Finding anything?" Logan asked, rubbing a towel through his hair.

I sighed and tossed my phone onto the bed. "No, nothing more than we already know. I think we should head to Switzerland. It's our best bet to find Andrew's family. I can check the library in Zurich, maybe check into some family history by way of the Department of Records."

"And where should I go?"

"To school," I answered.

Chapter 4

We arrived at the airport before the shops were open, which I didn't know was possible. Dragging my tired body to the gate made me hope this was the hardest part of my day. I'd slept last night, but my internal clock was off, and I was more tired now than I had been when we'd arrived. Logan stifled a yawn next to me as we found the coffee shop to be closed, so it seemed I wasn't the only one.

"I'll get breakfast once it opens," I offered, pulling him past the restaurant toward the gate. We dropped into our seats and tried to get as comfortable as possible. An hour passed, and I woke from the noise of people around us. Passengers were deboarding their planes while other people were gathering, ready for their flights. Logan was still sleeping, but I didn't want to miss our flights. We had decided it would be best if we took two separate flights to get there and stayed radio silent, just in case we were followed. Logan was flying to Zurich and heading right to Adelboden. I'd be flying to England first, where I'd hang out in some little town for a day or two before taking a flight to Zurich. The timeline depended on what research I found along the way.

Logan had been a godsend and booked our flights last night before we'd both passed out. My dad was depositing money for us into an account we each had access to. I was sure it was coming out of my college fund, but I didn't care.

I got up and joined the line of people waiting to place their breakfast orders. By the time it was my turn, I was nervous Logan would miss the first of our flights.

But two coffees and sandwiches later, Logan was on his plane, and I was looking for my gate. We said our goodbyes with a quick hug and my telling him to go for it with Bridget. All he did was blush.

The flight was about an hour and ten minutes, which I'd planned on sleeping through, but the coffee had hit my bloodstream, and I was wired. I turned on my phone and scrolled through messages I'd been ignoring. Hilary Thompson had sent me a gif of a giraffe snuggling a kitten. I smiled. This was our friendship, and it worked. Alec sent me a text asking how things were going, but I couldn't reply now. I left it alone and kept scrolling. My ex-girlfriend Kyle had sent me a Snapchat of her in her scorched graduation gown and throwing a peace sign and blowing kisses in response to the one I'd sent to her while getting ready that morning.

I closed the app and looked out the window. I really liked her, but she only dated me for status. Finding that out hurt more than I'd let on. People expected me not to feel deeply because I let them believe things didn't bother me, but it wasn't true.

I was glad to have been born with healing powers. It helped with the sting of pain, emotional or physical. I'd felt for Bridget when she'd learned Trip was dating her for the Amulet. Being used cut deeper than anything else. I hated that she'd had to go through it, too, but our misery loved company, and now she'd understand me better than anyone else. She'd be the only one.

My bladder was bursting by the time we landed, so I hit the bathroom as soon as I deboarded. I pretended to be lost as I came out to clear the space for anyone following or watching me, and then I aimed for the exit, breezing past baggage claim, glad for only having my carry-on. I wanted to turn my phone on and check in with Logan or Bridget, but I knew I couldn't until I was safe. Heading to the exit, I weaved in and out of people, hoping I didn't look like I was rushing too quickly or moving too slowly. Adjusting my backpack, I came upon the taxis, and I waved one down.

"Where are you going, young man?" the driver asked me. I faltered for a minute.

"To the town center," I said. I'd find a hotel easier there than here.

"Get in. Is this all you have?" she asked, opening my door.

"Yup. I travel light these days," I replied, climbing into the back seat. I settled in, buckled my seatbelt, and rested my bag on my lap.

My driver—Miriam, as per her displayed license—turned on her blinker and pulled into traffic.

"You from America?" she asked. Her accent was soft and comforting, giving me a warmth in my chest, a sense of calm, like getting a hug from a loved one.

"Yeah."

"First time here?" She stopped at a traffic light before making a right turn.

"In Ireland or Leeds?"

"Both."

"Um, first time to Leeds, but not to the UK." I looked out the window and watched other cars pass us on the road. My eyes were watching for any road signs so I could get my bearings.

"Do you like coming here?"

I debated my options. "I don't know. I just like traveling, I guess."

She smiled at me in the rearview mirror. "I'm from here, born and raised."

The conversation died out, and we remained silent for the rest of the ride. Miriam turned on the radio to a local channel and hummed along to a song I didn't recognize. It wasn't wholly unpleasant.

She pulled over and stopped by a park. Looking back at me, she said, "This is right next to the center of where you want to be."

"Where am I?"

"Yorkshire Dales National Park. That will be thirty-six pounds and forty pence."

I paid the fare and scrambled from the car.

"Thank you!" I said as I closed the door.

"Ta!" And she drove off, leaving me to my own devices. According to my phone, it was eleven in the morning, and I needed something else to eat. Those breakfast sandwiches had kept me going, but it was time to find some food and a place to crash. I could hold off on research for one day. Slipping my hands into my pockets, I headed toward what I thought were shops. Instead, I found a hiking trail that led me deeper into the fields. After a half hour of wandering, I arrived at an abstract structure that reminded me of a bird mid-flight, and I sat on a bench next to it. I needed directions, and I had to risk turning my phone on. Thank Brighde I wasn't far from a hostel on the property, based on my quick Google search, and they offered food. I felt rejuvenated and jumped up, following the arrows on my navigation app in combination with trail signs to the hostel.

By the time I arrived, it had been two hours after Miriam had dropped me off. I was exhausted, hungry, and in need of a shower. The weather was hotter than I'd anticipated, considering England was known for mild temperatures.

I located the entrance and walked in, letting my eyes adjust to the softer lighting.

"Hello, can I help you?" a girl a little older than me asked from behind a desk.

"Yes! Do you have any rooms available?" I moved closer but still kept my distance.

She typed something into her computer. "How many nights will you be staying?"

"Oh, two nights?" I didn't know what I'd be doing in two minutes, let alone in two days, but it sounded like the right answer.

"We have one room available for tonight, but you'd have to move tomorrow night. The first room is booked then."

"That's perfectly fine with me. Is there a place I can eat and shower?" I asked.

She smiled. "Yes. The private rooms have showers attached, and there's a burger and bar tent in the garden out back."

Nothing sounded better in that moment. "Great. Thank you."

"I'm Lacey, and I'll be here until half-past eight tonight if you need anything else." She rang me up and handed me a key. "Your room is up on the second floor, and this key will get you into it. The door here," she said as she nodded to the door I came in through, "is never locked, so this key won't help you out here."

"Thank you so much." I followed her directions down the hall and up the stairs to my room, number 203.

The room was clean and private, which was all I could ask for. I dumped my bag on the floor and pulled out my shower stuff. I wanted to eat, but it was vital I felt clean first. Grabbing a towel off the stack of linens, I wandered to the bathroom and hopped into the shower. The hot water rushed over me, and I never felt better. I washed off the sweat and dirt of the past two days as well as the plane and public transportation germs. When I was done, I dried off and put on the clothes I brought with me. The fresh scent put a little pep in my step as I left the bathroom. I headed back to my room, grabbed my key, and went out to find food.

No one seemed to be around when I walked up to the burger truck, which sucked considering how much I was salivating, but I was clean and not exactly in a hurry. I took in the landscape around me. There were rolling hills and deep valleys, stunning and picturesque, that belonged on a postcard or hanging in a doctor's office. If Bridget were here, she'd probably wax poetic about how pretty it all looked, but she wasn't, and it wasn't really my thing.

"Hello?" I called into the truck. No answer. I knocked lightly on the side. "Anyone there?" I called again.

"They may be on a wee break," a voice behind me said. Startled, I whipped around to face a stranger.

"Oh, I'm sorry! I didn't mean to scare ya," the person said.

"No problem," I said, giving them a quick smile. "Do you have any idea when they'll be back?"

"They usually take an hour, but that's only when they're slow. Like right now." They tucked their hands into their pockets.

"Oh, okay, thanks," I said, internally wishing I were close to a McDonald's or Wendy's.

"I have some crisps in my room if you'd like 'em. You seem like you need them more than me."

"That's really kind of you, but I can wait for the truck to reopen. Thank you, though," I said, stuffing my hands into my pockets.

"Well, if you change your mind, I'm on the third floor. Room 384." They walked off back toward the hostel, and I waited a few more minutes, hoping someone would come back and open up. No such luck, so I headed down the hill back to the main building.

Just as I was about to open the door, a bag was placed over my head, and my hands were pulled behind my back.

"You should have taken the crisps," they whispered in my ear.

I threw my body weight against them, hoping to knock them off balance. It worked, and we tumbled onto the concrete. My hands were freed, and I ripped the bag from my head. I ran to the other side of the building, hoping I'd make it inside to my phone, which I'd stupidly left in my room. Footsteps pounded heavily behind me, and I ducked behind a large dumpster and hoped they would move past. I was panting both in fear and from lack of cardio. I made myself silently breathe through my nose, even as I gulped air.

Their footsteps receded, and I waited an extra minute before moving from my spot. No one seemed to be around, so I quickly and quietly crept toward the back door. I prayed it wasn't locked, too. The knob turned, and I slipped inside. The room was thankfully empty, and I ran to the stairs and started thundering up them. After pulling my key from my pocket, I slid it into the lock, my heart pounding in my ears the whole time.

Hands on my shoulders dragged me off. I clawed at them, trying to twist away, but another pair of hands grabbed mine, and the bag was placed over my head again. I couldn't see anything. This time, someone tied my hands together while someone else grabbed my legs and tied my feet. I didn't even have a chance to topple before being slung over a shoulder, and something pricked my arm.

"Help! Someone help me!" I called, my voice muffled by the bag. I was slapped in the back of the head.

"Shut up. No one is here, so screaming is wasteful."

"Then why should I stop? Help!" I yelled again. This earned me another slap, harder than the last.

"Enough." Then I was pinched like we were on my elementary school playground.

"Ow!" If my hands weren't tied, I'd rub the spot.

I felt drowsy from what I knew was an injection. No way would I have felt so tired this quickly.

I did my best to fight against it, but soon, all I could remember was being carried from the hostel and closed in a car trunk before everything went dark.

Chapter 5

I woke as they dragged my drowsy body over the bumper of the car. I didn't know where I was or how long we'd been driving. *Holy* shit, did I hurt. I pushed my healing strength to my pounding head and to any bruises that bloomed under my skin. Relief and panic flooded my system as the healing worked its magic. It helped my brain feel less fuzzy after the dosing, which I greatly appreciated. My hands and feet were still bound as they carried me to wherever I was going.

Count the steps: There were thirty before we made a turn.

Remember the directions: One right turn.

Fifty steps.

Second right turn.

Twenty-five steps.

They dropped me onto the floor in a heap, sending pain through the whole left side of my body. My arms were pinched behind me, and I was struggling to get comfortable and end the aching.

The bag was ripped from my head, and the smell of hay and old manure rushed at me. I blinked and saw that I was in a dusty barn. There were no animals, but their shit was still here. Moldy hay and mouse droppings lay everywhere; the smell was overwhelmingly rank. Trying not to gag, I rolled over on some loose straw and groaned. Now there were two people blocking out the light, and I only recognized one of them.

Fucking Trip.

"Hi, Cay," he said, smiling. "How's it going?"

"Fuck you." I pushed myself up to a sitting position, pain be damned. "Is this some kind of tactic to get to Bridget?"

He *tsked* and shook his head. "No, Cay. Don't worry about Bridget. She's not your concern at this moment."

I sent a wave of healing down my whole body, and it kicked in immediately. "Then why am I here?"

"Remember what I said at graduation?"

"No. I don't think about you at all, really. You were there?" That earned me a kick in the ribs from Trip. I groaned and breathed through the deep discomfort as I healed the broken ribs. No one ever wanted to be jumped and kidnapped, but I thanked Brighde for my gift. It was a handy power to have when being beaten.

"Cay, Cay," Trip said, pacing in front of me with hands linked behind his back. "This would go a lot smoother if you didn't talk like you have no idea what's going on."

"But I'm so good at it." Another kick to the gut and another wave of healing. I could do this all day.

Trip stopped pacing and squatted to look me directly in the eye.

"You're going to tell me where Bridget keeps the Amulet."

I raised an eyebrow. "Oh, yeah? What's made you so sure about that?"

"I'll make you a deal. You tell me where the Amulet is, and I won't kill you."

Always with the dramatics. I barked out a laugh. "Please. You think that will loosen these lips?" Inching myself up, I relaxed against the hay and stretched out my bound legs.

He smiled. "I had to try."

"Why?"

Trip paused. "What do you mean?"

I wanted to gesture to my current state of being, but since my hands were bound behind me, I nodded my head to the disgusting space we were in. "You caught me. You know my loyalty is with my cousin. What made you think I'd change sides?" I shook my head. "You're not *that* stupid."

He didn't answer, then licked his lips and gulped.

Interesting. Doubling down, I pressed on. "You know we were both raised on a steady diet of hate and revenge, so who lied to you and said *I'd* be the weak link?"

"When did you become Dr. Phil?" Trip said, clearly deflecting.

I shrugged. "I watch a lot of TV."

He scoffed and shook his head. "If you have nothing to offer, then this conversation is over."

Trip looked back at the slimeball henchman who'd kidnapped me and then stood up. "You know what to do."

I gulped, mentally preparing myself for whatever would be coming my way. The henchman grabbed my right arm and hoisted me up. Wincing, I pushed off the ground, hoping to reduce the damage I'd have to fix later. Sometimes healing took a lot out of me, and I had a feeling I would soon need it in droves. Another henchman arrived, but this person was wearing a facemask and all-black clothing. There were no visible tattoos or markings on their hands, considering they were wearing gloves, and they wore generic black sneakers without a label. One pulled a switchblade from their pocket and cut the tape on my legs.

"Before you get any smart ideas," Trip started, "just know he will cut your femoral artery, and you'll bleed out before you even realize you've been injured."

Clearly, our little chat had done nothing for my future safety.

Seething, I didn't move or say anything. All I did was think of ways to kill Trip once I was free. Was drawing and quartering a person still a thing? If not, it would be making a comeback.

The second henchman poked me in the chest with the blade, forcing me back. Warm blood dripped down my torso to my stomach and soaked into the top of my pants. By the time they cut my hands free—if only to tie them together in front of me—I was healed.

I can do this all day, boys, I thought.

That feeling was short-lived as they lowered a chain, stuck a hook through the knot that bound my hands, and pulled a lever to lift the chain off the ground. It was just high enough to keep my feet from scraping the dirt on the floor, but my toes dragged as I swung back and forth.

"New deal," Trip started, pacing the floor again as the two goons headed toward the door to wait. "If you don't tell me what I want to know by the time I come back, I'll cut off a body part."

I shook my head in disbelief. "Fuck, man. I know we hate each other, but don't you think this is extreme? Cutting body parts off? We're eighteen! We shouldn't be doing shit like this!" Call me desperate, but I didn't want to lose limbs. Even if I could regrow a finger with my powers, I wasn't interested in finding out the hard way.

Trip stopped walking and looked at me. "I've never heard you swear this much."

"I really feel this moment calls for it," I replied, shrugging.

"You don't do it around Bridget."

I gritted my teeth. "She doesn't love it. If you knew her at all, you'd know that."

He ignored me and started pacing again. "As I was saying, don't answer my questions, and you'll lose a body part of your choosing."

"And I said, can we rethink this because that's fucking insane?"

He stopped walking again, looking at me once more. "Okay. I'll try something new you might take seriously: If you don't tell me where the Amulet half is by the time I come back, I'll find Bridget and kill her."

"You wouldn't."

Trip's smile spread slowly across his face, reminding me of the Joker.

"Try me."

Fucking Trip.

I tried to reach for him, struggling against the chain, but to no avail. Apparently, someone was in the Boy Scouts and got their badge for knot tying. "Leave her alone! Why play these war games? Just do your job and *search*!"

Shrugging, he answered, "The stakes have been raised."

"What the fuck does that mean?" I asked, squirming again.

"When I come back, I better have answers." With that, he turned and walked out, leaving me alone in a dark barn, hanging from a chain.

Fuck, fuck, fuck. *Think, Cay. What would Alec do?* I snorted. *Probably some smart martial arts move and just flip himself off this.* I looked up at the knot to see if it was frayed in any way. But its strands looked fresh and held together quite nicely. Grunting, I twisted my body again, hoping the third time would be the charm. All I did was tighten the knot. I hung there for a minute, trying to regroup. Maybe if I could swing my body back and forth with enough force to move the knot to the end of the hook, I'd slip it off. On tiptoe, I pushed myself backward and then forward, gaining momentum. As I swung freely in the air, I looked up only to see the knot didn't budge one centimeter.

I huffed out a grunt, and frustration set in with a dull ache in my shoulders. I sent some healing through, and the ache disappeared.

In a moment of desperation, I swung myself up again, this time getting my legs over my head to sling them over the hook. As I dangled, my pants slipped, and with my ass out for all the world to see,

I loosened the rope around my wrists. This gave me the slack to free the knot. Pulling on the outer loops, I had made it so tight that nothing was moving. Changing tactics, I tried to push it to the top of the hook, but I got it stuck on the bend, and I didn't have the strength to move it anymore. Another wave of frustration washed over me as I dropped my feet and took a breather. I sent more healing through as hunger and sleepiness set in.

What time was it? The walls were solid, allowing little to no light through, but based on the sunbeam coming through the gap under the door, it was later in the afternoon, maybe three or four o'clock, but my recent travels kept me from knowing if the sun was setting or rising. It was hard to focus when my stomach growled, demanding to be fed.

"I wish I may, I wish I might…" I muttered to myself. My mom used to say that to me when I begged her for a snack right before dinner. It gave me a minuscule drop of comfort. *They'll be back, and they'll have food or some kind of distraction to keep you from dwelling on how hungry you are.*

The door swung open, and the masked henchman came in with a bag. I perked up, hoping it was something to eat or drink. That dream was destroyed when he placed the bag over my head again and presumably left, indicated by the door slamming.

What good was the bag now? I'd already seen their faces, so hidden identity was less of a concern. Did that mean I was being reported officially dead? Why else would they put the bag on? I was awake and feeling trapped. I rubbed my head against my arm, trying to dislodge the itchy monstrosity on my head. It didn't work, and I wore my skin down, causing a scrape from all the rubbing, which I healed right away. Some loose thread tickled my nose, and I sneezed. It was the only thing that broke the silence in the barn.

The bag smelled of musty potatoes. It wasn't particularly appetizing, but I instantly thought of the mashed potatoes my family made during the holidays. I wished it was Thanksgiving and that there were loads of food on the table. Turkey, yams, green bean casserole, the rolls. Oh, the rolls. Forget the pumpkin pie; I was all about the rolls. I wished I could devour it all.

My shoulders ached again, so I healed them over. With the lack of food and water, I was draining more quickly, and I needed to reserve my healing.

Don't think about food. Think about anything else besides food. My stomach howled in protest, but I had no choice. I needed a different distraction.

I wondered if Brighde had telepathic powers. If I tried to contact Bridget with my mind, would she hear me?

It was worth a shot. *<Bridget! Bridget, help! Mayday! I'm... somewhere, kidnapped by Trip. I need rescuing!>*

I waited a minute, but no one replied. It felt obvious, but what else could I do with my time? My body was feeling increasingly tired as the weight of it pulled on my shoulders. The ache was back, exhaustion tugging at my bones and nibbling on my muscles, but I couldn't do much more.

I heard the door open again, and hope bloomed in my chest. I turned my head to follow the footsteps I heard, but I couldn't tell who it was. They had a clean walk, no shuffling or dragging, which was the only identifiable thing about them at the moment. No one came over to me.

"Hey!" I called through the fabric of the bag. "Can I get some food?"

No response, but I knew they were there because they stopped walking.

"Or water?" I heard two footsteps toward me, a squeak, and then another step. It took me a second to recognize the sound of a water pump. I didn't notice it before being inside the barn, but I *was* a little distracted. I heard the water gush into a metal container, and I felt better knowing I would get to drink something. They closed the pump with another squeak, and I heard them splash water. Maybe they were putting it in a cup for me? Or maybe they'd take me down to drink. I was open to either option.

Instead, they let it sit there, toying with me, as the footsteps headed to my right. Then they left, shutting the barn door behind them.

Fucking assholes.

I must have dozed off, though it seemed impossible, because when the door opened again, no light filtered through the bag. The room was dark until someone turned on an overhead light, and I flinched. My mouth felt dry and sticky from lack of hydration, and I thought back to the water. I idly wondered if they had emptied it, or if the crystal-blue water was still sitting there, waiting for me to take a sip.

The light went off as the door shut, and I was alone again.

This pattern continued for hours. Someone would come in, turn the light on, move around or adjust the water, turn off the light, and leave. Even when I fell asleep, I'd be jolted back by the lack of feeling in my shoulders. I kept sending healing waves to them and my arms, which had probably lost all blood by now, but that was getting harder to maintain. I needed food or water to restore myself. With nothing else to do, I fell asleep again.

Some hours later, someone came in and removed my bag. I blinked at the sudden light, but it was the henchman who'd lured me away from the burger tent back at the hostel.

"The fuck do you want?" I asked them as my stomach made a dull grumble.

"Nothing. Just checking in. Do you want to give up the location of the Amulet or Bridget?"

"Nope. Want to give me something to eat or drink?"

"Nope." The bag went back on, and they walked off, leaving the light on.

The next morning, I think, the bag came off again, and my head rolled forward. I had no energy to hold myself up, the weight of my body pulling on my arms and my legs hanging lifelessly underneath me. I sent whatever healing I could to my upper body, and that helped enough for me to breathe a sigh of relief.

"Are you ready to give up the location of the Amulet or Bridget?" The masked henchman was asking.

"No. Are you ready to feed me?"

"Nope." He left, leaving the bag off. I almost called out in thanks.

Water was being poured in the stall across from me. The trough hung on the wall. It had no legs under it for support, and there was a spigot right above it. They had filled the trough to the brim, pieces of hay and dirt floating in what spilled over the edge. I didn't care. I'd drink it happily if I could get off this hook.

The door opened again, and this time, Roden came in. I must have shown my surprise because he said, "Happy to see me?"

"Depends. Are you going to give me a sip of water?" I croaked.

He grinned like Trip. "Not unless you want to tell me where the Amulet is."

"Just that? Not Bridget too?"

He shook his head. "She's not important to me."

"Well, in that case… no," I said, moving my body to avoid numbness.

"I don't know if you remember, Cay, but you used to torture me in high school." Roden sauntered over to me slowly, his arms swinging by his side as he waited for my answer. He clenched his hands into fists, and alarms went off in my head.

I sighed. "It wasn't personal. I was trying to show Bridget her destiny."

Without warning, he punched me right in the stomach. I grunted and scrunched my body the best I could while hanging from a chain.

"That was for the dance." He punched me again, this time in my kidney. I arched my back, hoping to deflect some of the pain. "That was for setting Logan up to steal my date."

I lifted my legs to kick him, but I was too weak to do any damage. He laughed at me.

"Oh, you're pathetic. Can't even fight back?"

"Let me off this hook, and I'll show you what I can do," I threatened. Roden laughed again.

"You can try, but you're so weak, you probably can't even stand."

I couldn't argue with him because he was probably right. I looked away, focusing on a piece of hay on the floor.

"Whatever," he scoffed. "If you don't have any answers, then I can't help you."

I scoffed back as best as I could. "Help me? What here is helpful?" The chain jingled above my head. My hands were twisted in the rope that bound them together, which was getting more and more painful. I absent-mindedly sent some healing to them.

Roden shook his head. "This could end if you tell me where the Amulet is."

"Never."

"Then this conversation is over." He punched me in the face, and I heard the bones in my nose break. I sent every atom of healing to my nose, but the process was beyond slow. The blood dripped down my face, into my mouth, and down my chin. I spit it out on the floor by Roden's feet.

"That was just for fun," he said before putting the bag over my head and walking out.

He was the last person to come into the barn for another two days.

Chapter 6

Cay? Cay?

I rolled my head up and blinked, forgetting the cover over my head. In the filtered light, I didn't see anyone else, but I heard my name being called.

Cay, wake up! I'm coming!

"Who? Bridget? Is that you?"

Yes, Cay. I'm on my way.

I sighed in relief as my eyes closed again. "Can you bring me a snack when you show up?"

I'll bring you my mom's chocolate chip cookies.

I smiled. Cookies were always an excellent choice and my personal favorite.

"See you soon," I drawled as I passed out.

A little while later, I jerked awake as someone ripped the bag off my head.

Deidra. Her hair was pulled into a high ponytail, making her look even more evil than normal. She had two people with her, but I didn't recognize them.

She snapped her fingers, and her minions lifted me off the hook. I fell onto the floor, crashing pathetically into a lump. I'd relied on my healing to keep me going, but I couldn't sustain it anymore. My body hurt worse than I'd ever experienced. I rubbed my shoulders as best as I could with my hands still tied, and blood pooled into my arms and down from my hands. Numbness had already set in, despite my best efforts. My stomach churned, and I doubled over, dry heaving.

Deidra sighed and threw a bag at me. "You're so dramatic. Here."

After my spasm calmed, I tenderly picked up the bag in case it was a trap. At this point, I wouldn't have put it past any of them.

Opening it, I smelled sweet, freshly baked bread. At first, I flipped it around, looking for any signs of tampering, but my brain screamed to eat it and deal with it later, so I took a bite and chewed. It was like glue in my mouth, but I'd never been happier.

"Good to know you're so trusting," Deidra sneered.

I swallowed, painfully, and took another bite. "I'll take my chances."

A chair appeared, and I lazily wondered if it had always been there, or if I was hallucinating. Deidra scraped it across the floor, swirling up dust and debris. I coughed and wished—not for the first time since being kidnapped—for water. My stomach roiled at the feeling of food in it, but I ignored it and took another bite.

"Look, McKay," she said, sitting in the chair and leaning forward, "I'm not the monster everyone thinks me to be. I don't want you to die."

"Funny way of showing it," I said around a mouthful of food. Something buzzed into the forefront of my mind about how I shouldn't rush eating, but I didn't care. Hunger was real, and I could be dead any second. Who knew if this was the last time I'd eat?

"I know, I know. My bad with Bridget," Deidra said, sitting back. "But you have to agree she was wrong."

My mouth reminded me of the Sahara Desert, so I croaked, "I'll agree to anything if I can have a cup of water."

She snapped her fingers, and one of the minions handed me a bottle.

"Oh, fancy," I said, cracking open the drink. The first sip tasted like success mixed with angel tears. Like I'd survive this. Trying to salvage what I'd been given, I forced myself to stop after downing half the bottle. Too much too soon would overwhelm me and make myself worse.

"Now, you got your water, and you got your bread. It's your turn," Deidra said, leaning forward and resting her forearms on her legs.

Wariness blanketed me, my body sick and sleepy all at once. I didn't care what she wanted. I wanted to eat, drink, sleep, and leave, but not in that order.

"Go on."

I looked up at her and blinked slowly. "Before I agree, what am I saying she's wrong about?"

An irritated sigh slipped from her lips, and her nostrils flared while her blonde ponytail swung against her back.

"She was wrong for not telling us about the Amulet."

"Are you sure that's it?" I shook my head and immediately regretted what I'd said. "I don't think that's what she's wrong about." I pressed a dirty hand to my forehead and willed my body to heal *something*. Instead, it allowed the dull aches I had collected to sing in harmony as they each caused pain and reminded me of their existence.

She crossed her legs and leaned back, relaxed as could be.

What I wouldn't have given for a shower. I could stand smelling a little longer. Bridget was on her way. Or had I made that up? Doubt crept in, and I didn't like it.

"We both know what I'm talking about, so quit playing games."

Unsure if it was the little bit of sustenance I'd had or pure gumption, but I whipped my head up to look at her.

"You're fucking *kidding*, right?" I threw both hands up and scoffed in disbelief as I shook my head. Looking at the minions, I said, "Can you believe her? She says *I'm* playing games?"

They, of course, kept quiet, and she folded her arms across her chest and looked down at me from her perch.

"Cay, you understand what's at stake here, don't you?"

It took everything in my power not to jump up and punch her. We weren't supposed to resort to violence, but that ship had sailed and was currently on the ocean floor.

"No. Then explain it to me," I said hotly.

"Oh," she clucked her tongue and pressed two fingers to her lips. "This is a little awkward. I was told you were clear on the directions. You don't want Trip to come in here, do you?"

Trip's words echoed in my head. *"If you don't tell me where the Amulet half is by the time I come back, I'll find Bridget and kill her."*

I narrowed my eyes at her and said nothing as I bit into the bread, chewed, and swallowed. I repeated the action three more times, and by the end, I'd almost finished the loaf. As I took a sip from the bottle, Deidra launched herself from the chair and slapped it from my hands. It skittered away, water sloshing out. No one moved until I raised my eyes to meet hers. If I was developing any new powers, now would be the time to try them out. I was hoping for fire or laser vision.

"I hope you got your fill. You're done for now." With a flick of her wrist, the minions grabbed me from under my arms and dragged me to a stall before tying me to a rung on the door.

"How's Cole?"

Deidra's face fell as the minions backed away. She didn't answer as she crossed her arms over her chest and pushed out her hip. *Yahtzee.*

"Heard from him lately?"

"Fuck you, Cay" was her response.

"Yeah, yeah. *I'm* the problem here, but you were the one who left him high and dry right before winter break. I wonder how that made him feel." Never had I been happier to have paid attention to Bridget's gossip.

She dropped her hands to her sides and leaned toward me. "You *are* the problem. If you don't help us, then I can't help you."

Before I could come back with one of my classic remarks, Deidra strutted out. Then the lights were turned off, and the door slammed shut, echoing in the silence I was left in.

It didn't matter. I'd had just enough to start healing. I sent waves of it throughout my body, attempting to repair what I could.

Nothing happened.

I tried again, and panic bubbled in my chest when it failed. My healing had *never* failed. *Calm down and try again.* I did, concentrating on the worst parts first: my shoulders to restore strength, my arms to return the feeling, my organs to not give up functioning. The slightest feeling came back to my arms, but nothing else restored. I gulped and sank against the door.

If my healing failed, I was more fucked than ever.

I must have fallen asleep because the next thing I knew, loud music was blasting through the barn. Shocked awake, I searched for the culprit in the pitch-black darkness, the only light coming in from the moon through the door. I couldn't see anyone or anything, but the music continued. Uncomfortable pressure built in my ears, and I pressed them against my upper arms to counter the pain. Just as it had started, the music abruptly stopped. The ringing in my ears was the only sound for a long time. I was able to calm down enough to fall asleep, but then the music started again. I gave up and just rested my head back. *She will come, she will come, she will come...*

The next time someone came in, I was given another small loaf of bread and a bottle of water. I didn't know what day it was, but it was early morning based on the twilight pouring in behind them. I stopped recognizing the lackeys who came in and out, and I was untied every time I was given food but was never allowed to finish the bottle of water. Either they ripped it out of my hands or knocked it out, and I eventually lost the will to fight or be snarky. My body and mind were in a constant state of fatigue. The hope Bridget would figure it out and come and get me was the only thing keeping me going. I wanted to cry, but I was too dehydrated. All I could do was sit there and feel sorry for myself.

What felt like days later, Trip came back in.

"Get him up," he instructed his henchman. They untied me and hauled me to my feet, standing directly in front of the prick in charge.

"I wouldn't get too close to me. I haven't been keeping up with my personal hygiene these days." I felt weak and wanted to waver, but I was being held up by his followers.

"This is your last chance, McKay. Where is Bridget keeping the Amulet?" His eyes were narrowed, and he had dark circles. His shirt was less pressed and clean than normal, and he kept flexing his jaw.

"Problems at home?" I asked. "You look like you could use some sleep. I suggest that pile of straw over there." I nodded. "It's the comfiest pile here."

Trip let out a frustrated groan and turned away. He breathed heavily for a minute and then spun on his heel, pointing his finger at me.

"You don't know who you're dealing with. Tell me where the Amulet is, and I can save us all."

I frowned. If it wasn't him running this shitshow, who was? "If this is your idea of saving me, we need to work on your definition of the word."

He shook his head and muttered to himself. "The two of you... so ridiculously stupid."

The two of us? Maybe I wasn't the only one hallucinating. Were there other captives here?

"Just know," Trip said, looking at me with wet, dull eyes, "This is on you. I tried."

This tender, caring Trip was not what I was used to and was probably just another torture tactic.

"Try harder?" I wanted to sound demanding, but it came out as a plea. At this point, I probably was pleading.

Trip looked at me, a muscle in his jaw flexing. Without a word, he jerked his thumb behind his shoulder, and his goons shoved me toward the hook, where I stumbled and fell into the hay. Before I could recalibrate, they grabbed my hands and slapped metal cuffs onto them.

This was new. The hook was lowered, and the chain between the cuffs was looped through it.

Internally, I groaned. The hook would hurt even more now with the metal cuffs digging into my wrists. The sharp sensation of my shoulder joints being pulled at punishing angles was back, and I couldn't ease it. Trip disappeared in a hurry, leaving the light on, but he closed the door and locked it.

I hung there for hours. With the light on, I couldn't sleep. It bothered my brain just enough to keep it awake and spinning in circles. The cuffs did their job and cut into me brutally. The slicing of my skin was torturous as blood dripped down my arms. I tried to think of my happy place, but I couldn't get there anymore, so I stared at a spot on the floor, where my daily bread lay. A mouse came sniffing out from a crack in the wall and searched around for something. I watched as he discovered and nabbed my bread. He took a nibble and chewed furiously before grabbing the rest of the hunk and dragging it back to wherever he'd come from. Maybe he was going to feed his little mouse family. Maybe he would eat it all in one go, or he'd save it for a week. Either way, I smiled at the thought. At least something good had come from my capture.

ChapteR
7

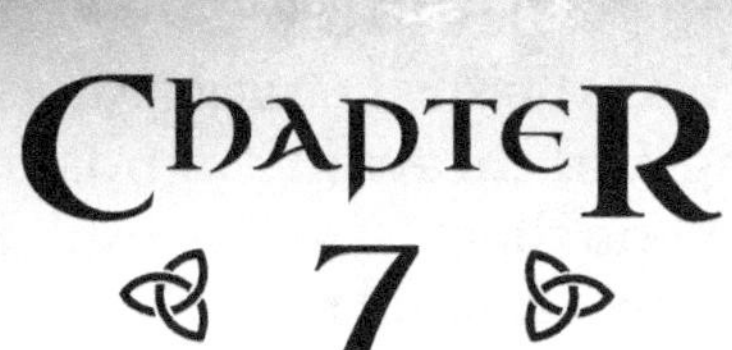

I must have passed out again because I awoke with my hands sticky with blood. My body was heavy, sore, tired, and numb. The barn door creaked open as a figure crept in. Blue morning light followed them in, casting a shadow. I didn't move to avoid drawing attention, but I followed them with my eyes. The figure tiptoed to where I hung and dropped something at my feet. I heard a little metal tinkle. They turned and quietly hurried out, closing the door as softly as they could behind them.

I looked down and was able to make out what was left behind.

A key.

Hope grew in my body in a way I hadn't experienced in a long time. Craning my neck, I looked up to see how I was attached to the hook. Like a clasp on a necklace, the hook was slid into one link. I bet if I swung again and lifted myself like I had the first time, I could use the force to slide it off. Ignoring searing pain, I moved my body like a playground swing, using my legs for momentum. Mid-swing, I pulled my hands forward hard enough to get the loop to slide up the curve. On my way back, the loop slid back down to the valley of the hook. I didn't want to give up. This was the first chance of escape I'd had. Again, I swung and threw my hands forward. I got farther, but still no dice. Urgency built inside me, as I didn't know who'd helped me or if I'd be discovered. I wanted to be gone before anyone noticed.

I kept trying, getting closer with each swing. Heat radiated from my body with the exertion, but I was too dehydrated to sweat. My body worked against me, wanting me to rest, to quit, but I couldn't. I had to make this happen. I swung again and mustered up all the force I could with my hands, throwing my body weight with it. The hook dipped down, and the loop slid forward, freeing itself from the point. I fell, landing on my knees. I didn't care about the aches and, instead, focused on hunting for the key in the dirt. It was under my leg, and I grabbed it, then tried to find the lock on the cuffs. The metal clanged loudly as I placed the key into the hole and twisted it. The cuffs sprung open. My wrists immediately felt better, even if they were still raw. I rushed to the door and paused, listening for footsteps or sounds. Hearing nothing, I pushed it open, finally seeing where I'd been for days. Weeks? Years?

I hugged the side of the barn and tried to remember the direction I'd come from. Nothing looked familiar in the morning twilight, but it didn't matter. I was lost in a foreign country; nothing would look familiar. I stayed low to the ground and headed to the right. Stopping to peek around the corner, I determined the area looked clear. All around the barn was farmland, and I didn't know where I could get away or how.

A cluster of trees was in the distance on the other side of the farm. None of the Findlays would think I'd go there, so I waited to hear that no one else was up and booked it as fast as I could across the field. Being weak, sore, and malnourished was not usually recommended for this type of exercise, but my life was on the line, and I needed to get to Bridget. Fuck the lead I'd found. We could regroup when I got to her.

If I found her. *Was she still on her way?*

Panic resurfaced immediately. If she came here, and I wasn't here, what would Trip do to her? Was I putting her in danger? I *had* to find her first, before she found me.

My heart pounded in my chest as I dove behind a tree trunk. I listened for any indication I'd been caught now that the sun was higher in the sky and the blue moonlight was burned off. There wasn't a peep from any animal or human. Once my breathing calmed, I pushed through to the next farm. Horses were in the far part of the pasture. Keeping to the trees as much as possible, I skirted around the fence line. I'd seen enough YouTube videos to know the animals would charge if an intruder entered their space. My body wouldn't survive being trampled by a quadruped.

A bird took flight, its feathers brushing against the leaves and knocking a few off. I flinched and ducked, fearing I would be found. No one was around except a farmer in the distance. Not wanting to take the chance, I melted into the trees and continued away from my captors.

I had no idea where I was going. I climbed stone walls and crossed another field or two before I came to a road. Unsure of which direction I should head in, I walked left, positioning the barn and Trip behind me. After about fifteen minutes of walking, I came upon a sign that said "Bramhope 10.81 km" with an arrow pointing back the way I had just come from. I didn't know if that I meant I was getting closer to Bridget or further from Trip and his merry band of psychopaths, but I knew I couldn't go back that way. I kept walking, hoping to find a river or something to drink and a place to hide and rest.

The sun was high, indicating it was nearly noon, if my wilderness skills could be counted on. I needed to recuperate, but I was in the middle of a country road. If the road signs were any help, I was coming up on a town called Bolton Abbey. As I trudged along, I kept thinking of the things I'd do when I finally made it to Bridget. Showering and sleeping were at the top of my list. Throw in a meal, and I'd be good. My cuts had scabbed over and were unsightly with the bloody sleeves. My blue shirt was dirty and had sweat stains, and my shorts were torn. My feet hurt, and I couldn't do anything to stop it. I found some shade under a tree and sat, giving myself a break. *A small one.* As I rested, I thought back to what had brought me here, and it wasn't a great walk down memory lane. I focused on taking full breaths, even if it killed me.

After a few minutes, I rallied and dragged my body up and onto the road to continue to Bolton Abbey. After another hour, I saw signs indicating the town limits for my destination, and I almost cried. Crossing the borders, I kept going until I found a hotel and walked in.

"Hello," I said, walking up to the front desk. I kept my arms crossed over my chest, hoping to hide most of the blood. Thankfully, some of it had flaked off on my walk.

"Yes, sir?" the woman said.

"Is there a public toilet I could use?"

She looked me up and down with concern, probably wondering what the hell I'd been through.

"Right around the corner, to your left," she directed. I thanked her and followed her instructions. No one was in the bathroom, so I hurried over to the sink and washed my hands. As the water flowed, I ducked my head under the faucet and drank until my empty stomach was full, though I risked making myself sick. I used a paper towel and wiped my face, smearing dirt around. Washing the blood off my hands and arms, I saw my cuts that were definitely *not* healing. Using the hand soap, I scrubbed my face and used more paper towels to dry off. Short of washing my hair, I did the best I could for a birdbath. I felt a little better being cleaner and fresher. My teeth felt grimy, but I ignored it and drank more water to dull the hungry ache.

When I left the washroom, I slipped quietly through the lobby while making sure to avoid the concierge. She was assisting another customer, so I made a quick getaway. As I walked outside, I saw a tourist center across the street, so I headed that way and picked up a map of the trails surrounding the town. They had one for Yorkshire Dales National Park where the hostel was.

My body trembled, remembering my abduction. Would they find me there again? My stuff was hopefully still there, so I could get my phone or use a computer.

I looked up and down the street. Was there a library? I could use their computer to find my phone and send a message to Logan or Bridget.

My pulse jumped. Has Logan made it to her? What if he's been caught, too? Fear took over, and I melted into the shadows on the building. *Please, Brighde, let Logan and Bridget be safe. Even if I'm not.*

Crumpling to the ground, I tucked my ankles under my legs in a crisscrossed position, staying out of the sun and hiding in the shadows. I didn't want to move anymore, but I couldn't stay here. It wasn't safe.

I was stuck.

Stop. This isn't what Bridget would want for you. This isn't what you were meant to do. Your dad loves you. Alec loves you. So do Logan and Bridget. You have to keep going for them. I looked at the wrinkled guide in my hand. I could do this. I had to do this.

Hostel. Get my stuff. Go to Switzerland. Find Bridget.

I stood and slid the map into my back pocket. Checking one more time that no one was following, I left the tourist center and walked on the edge of the main road; I hoped I wouldn't be spotted.

According to the map, I was about eight kilometers from the park and another eleven from the hostel. Feeling a little more hopeful and determined than I had an hour ago, I followed signs to the park and headed out of town.

About two and a half hours later—by my guess—I made it to the park and almost cried. I had reached an unbearable level of dehydration, and I needed to eat and sleep more than ever. *Just keep going. Almost there.* Trip had to know I was gone already and had probably launched a full-scale attack on Bridget or a hunt to find me. Panic spiked as I realized it could have been his plan all along. Had I escaped by accident, or had it been an anticipated eviction?

I swallowed the fear. *No time for anything but focusing.* I entered the trail path and walked into the bosom of the forest. The birds chirped as if singing to me, encouraging me to keep going, while squirrels chased each other down trunks and across tree limbs alongside me. Despite the cheerful song the birds sang out loud, I understood how the chased squirrel felt—I couldn't shake the pinpricking, creepy feeling I was being followed, even if I ignored it. I smiled at the squirrel's determination to keep going and made a conscious effort to keep putting one foot in front of the other, no matter how much they hurt. I dreaded taking off my shoes to see the damage.

I heard voices up ahead and gulped, jumping into a bush, hoping they would think I was an animal. The other hikers walked past, not looking in my direction at all. I waited until they were beyond the bend before I let out my breath.

Chill out, Cay. People walk this path all the time. No one dangerous knows you're here. I continued my journey, hurrying along as much as I could. I wasn't sure how long it had been, but I finally came up on the hostel and was torn between fearing someone was waiting for me and being happy to get my stuff back … if it was still there.

People were filtering into the building, some holding grocery bags. Maybe it was around dinner time. My stomach howled thinking of it.

How would I get past everyone looking like this? It didn't matter. I needed to get in, get my stuff, shower, and get some sleep. I'd beg for food if I had to. Taking a deep breath, I forged ahead and pushed away my fear when I touched the doorknob to the entrance. I looked around, but no one was in the shadows. I walked inside to the sound of silverware clinking against plates down the hall. A different person from before was behind the desk when I approached. An older gentleman with glasses and graying hair, he looked kind, but I had learned the hard way that looks could be deceiving.

"Um, hi," I said, keeping my hands out of sight.

His eyes widened when he looked up at me. "Can I help you?"

"Yeah. I'm a guest here, and I wanted to get my stuff."

"Name?" He sat up, ready to type my name into the computer.

"Cay McKay."

The guy moved his hands away from the computer. "I remember your name. I'm sorry, but your things aren't here anymore. Your friend came and picked them up for you."

The blood drained from my face as my stomach dropped, and the underlying vein of fear burst, coating my tongue with panic.

"What friend?"

"I don't think we got a name, but he was here the day after you left and grabbed your bag."

"How long ago was this?" I swallowed back the bile slowly creeping up my throat.

"About a month ago."

A month. I'd been Trip's prisoner for a month, had been starved and tortured, and no one had noticed.

"Oh. Okay," I said weakly. I couldn't stay here. Even if they didn't think I'd be back, someone could be babysitting this place just in case. I drifted away from the desk while scanning the room for anyone else.

"Wait!" The guy turned around and grabbed a box of lost and found. "I believe someone found a phone on the floor of your room when they were cleaning it. Is this yours?"

He pulled out the only phone in the box, my iPhone with the blue case. It was either off or dead, but I had options. A T-shirt and a pair of shorts were also in the box.

"Thank you. Um, are those clothes claimed?" I pointed to the items.

"No," he answered.

"Could I borrow them?" I looked down at my clothes, which were a mess.

"I'm sure that would be fine. Do you need something else? A room?" he asked while taking out the clothes. I didn't know if they'd fit, but I didn't give a shit. Clean clothes were clean clothes.

"No, thank you." I collected my phone and the clothes and walked out, trying to remember where I'd seen another hostel in the park. Not wanting to be as visible, I stayed away from the light in the parking lot. After pulling the map from my back pocket, I let the filtered light show me what other lodgings were nearby. Luck was on my side, finally, as there was a pub and hotel just down the road. My feet rejoiced at the idea of not walking much longer, even if I could do nothing else to soothe them for the time being.

Folding the map back up and tucking it away, I scanned to make sure I was still alone before I made my way to the main road. As I walked toward the town center, I stayed behind stone fences and ducked any time a car passed. My heart thudded in my chest each time I saw the glow of headlights, and I pressed against the stones while wondering if passersby would see me. I listened to every noise I could think of, my ears straining to hear every little sound all at once.

It felt like forever before I made it within the marketplace limits where doors were shuttered up and down the road. I had no idea what time it was with a dead phone, so I stopped behind a mailbox to pull out the map again. According to the guide, the hotel wasn't too far away. Clutching my belongings under my arm, I made my way down the street, whipping around every time I thought I heard footsteps. Cars lined the street, giving the impression every person in town was home for the night. As I walked past cars, my tired muscles tensed, expecting someone to jump out at any moment.

The entrance to the hotel took me by surprise, and I nearly passed it. Taking one more scan of the road around me, I scurried inside to the main desk, rang the bell, and hoped someone was around.

"Hello, can I help you?" an older woman asked as she came around a corner. She had graying hair tied in a ponytail and was wearing a sweater that made me desperately wish for clean and warm clothing of my own.

"Do you have a room available?" I asked feebly. I eyed her warily, unsure if she could be trusted.

"We may," she said, walking up to the computer. "Are you alright?" She eyed my soiled, smelly clothes, making me feel uneasy. I tugged at my dirty shirt with my free hand.

"I was hiking earlier today and fell into the mud by one of the waterfalls. Someone took my bag but left these clothes," I pointed to a ball of fabric under my arm, "and my phone. Which is now dead."

"You poor thing! You're lucky to have made it here. We have a room available. I'll need to see some ID to book it and get you all set."

I looked at her sheepishly. "My ID was in the bag that was taken."

"Oh, that's horrible. Have you notified the local constabulary?"

"Not yet."

"Alright then, love, let's see what I can do for you. Do you have a credit card?"

"If you had a charger, I could pull up payment on my phone."

She gave me a tight smile. "Normally we don't accept payment like that, but I think we can work with you on this. I'll be right back, dear."

I looked around, noting I was utterly alone. Something told me she didn't believe me, and

I backed away from the desk while frantically checking if anyone else would suddenly appear.

I made it to the door when she returned. "I found the cord for an iPhone, but I wasn't sure if you had—" She stopped. "Did you forget something?"

I gulped. "No."

"Well, like I said, I found a charger if you'd like to borrow it. Do you have an iPhone?"

Everything inside me was screaming to leave, but I couldn't. Shakily, I headed back to the desk and handed her my dead phone.

"Wonderful. I'll plug this in for a minute to charge. In the meantime, would you like something to eat? Our kitchen is almost closing, but we could whip up a little something for you."

"Sure. Thank you," I said.

"Follow me," she said. She came out from around the desk and headed into another room. There were a few other people there—some were drinking at the bar, and there was a couple at one of the tables. The hotel concierge led me to a table against a wall, away from the other patrons. I sat facing the rest of the room and placed my clothes and the map on the seat next to me. She grabbed a menu from above my head and handed it to me.

"Have a look and let me know what you'd like. I'll bring you a glass of water." She left me alone, and I swallowed hard as I tore my eyes away from the other patrons to review the menu. It was mostly tea with sandwiches. I didn't care what I'd be eating. It would be better than nothing. Than the dry bread. Bile rose in my throat thinking of it, and I willed the contents to go back down. I didn't know if I could ever eat bread again.

She returned with a large pint of water, which I grabbed and took a large gulp of. My brain told me not to down it, but I fought against the urge. Health class had taught us not to chug water after days of dehydration or we'd get sick. They never told us how hard it would be to resist the impulse.

"Have you decided?" she asked me.

"Um, do you have anything that isn't a sandwich?" I asked hopefully, taking another gulp of water and placing it back down.

"I'll see if we can make something else." She left me again, and I stared at the room, making myself drink the water slowly.

It was a quaint space, the wall a dark green that clashed with the flowered tablecloths. The tables and chairs didn't match, as if they'd grabbed a spare chair from another set once one of them had broken.

I leaned against the back of the chair, grateful my back was against the wall with how vulnerable and exposed I felt. By the time she came back with a plate of pasta, my pint of water was empty. She placed the food in front of me and whisked my glass away without a word. Wondering if it could be tainted, I stared at the food for a minute. There was no time like the present to find out. The food smelled good, drenched in red sauce with cheese on top. The first bite was perfect on my tongue, but my stomach revolted, and I had to take a minute to adjust. I chewed slowly, taking my time before swallowing. When nothing instantaneous happened, I took another bite and ate carefully, still not wanting to make myself sick.

The woman came back with another glass of water and my phone.

"It appears to have charged to thirty-five percent. I didn't think you'd want to delay turning it on any further."

I gave her a tight smile and nodded, then pressed the button and waited for the screen to light up.

Once I turned off airplane mode, message after message came through. Logan, my dad, my friends from OCHS, Alec. I checked the ones from Logan first. He'd made it to Zurich, and Bridget was safe. I breathed a sigh of relief.

"It's working." I opened my mobile wallet since I didn't have the physical one with me. "I can book a room and pay for the food."

"When you're finished here, come up to the front desk, and we can get you settled." She smiled warmly at me and left me alone again.

I ate and sipped, forcing myself not to rush. If my healing was on the fritz, I didn't want to make it worse.

The bar emptied out, leaving me and the two bartenders left. My nerves jumped, and I pushed my half-eaten dish away from me. The food was uncomfortably heavy in my stomach, so I packed it. Making sure no one else was near, I slipped out of the dining room and headed back to the main desk.

The old woman from reception was waiting at the desk for me. "Ready?"

Keeping an eye on the dining room door, I nodded and waited for further instructions. After a few clicks of the mouse and some typing on the keyboard, the woman said, "I booked you the private suite. It's the only room available, and we had a cancellation this morning. You can shower and rest up there."

"Do you have any shower stuff, or a toothbrush?" I asked her.

She smiled. "The room is fully stocked with all the toiletries needed. I just need a card to book the room."

I slid over my phone and let her type in the card information. I knew this was a huge risk, but I was stuck and didn't have any other options.

When finished, she handed my phone back. "Will you need anything else?"

"May I borrow the charger a little longer?" I asked.

"Only for a bit. This is one of the chef's personal chargers." She gave me a key assigned to room 314 along with the charger.

"I'll be quick with it," I assured her. I was numb to everything, dissociated and watching myself. I needed to get out of here.

"Thank you." I saw the staircase across from a swinging door and headed toward it. Climbing the stairs to the third floor, I held the borrowed clothes close to my chest. As I reached the door to my room, I slid the key into the lock and opened it. Once inside, I let out a shaky breath. Immediately, I closed the door, locked it, then dumped the clothes onto the bed. I was tired of feeling so ... scared.

The first thing I did was plug my phone back in. I wanted to get as much of a charge as I could before someone came looking for the charger. Next, I sat on the floor and gingerly removed my shoes and socks. My feet were blistered and covered in bloody sores. No wonder I'd been in so much pain. The socks used to be white, but now they were streaked with dirt and blood, causing a kaleidoscope of grime on the bottom. I stood and stripped, peeling off the grimy clothes and wincing as the pieces of fabric tore from my body like bandages from a bloodied injury. I never wanted to see or wear these things again. I had rashes from living in the same clothes for weeks without getting clean. Bruises dotted my legs; they were already becoming welts beginning to heal. The ropes had cut cruelly into my wrists, leaving thick imprints in my skin as the cuts crusted over.

I got a whiff of myself and was ashamed thinking about how badly I'd smelled when talking to the nice woman.

After taking the supplies to the bathroom, I turned on the hot water and dumped everything into the stall. Steam rose in tendrils, and I stepped in. Flinching from the water and the burning on my injuries, I took my time lathering. First my hair, then my body. As I rinsed off, I looked down at the water, watching the dirt swirl at my feet and go down the drain. I stayed standing until the water ran clean. Once I got out and dried off, I noticed how scratchy the towel was against my wounds. Pulling on the new clothes, I heard a knock at my door. My heart dropped, and I pressed myself against the wall behind the door.

I slowly counted to five before forcing myself to move. I peered through the peephole, and a guy carrying a chef's jacket was standing outside.

"Yes?" I asked, grabbing a pen from the guestbook.

"I'm the chef, and Kay told me you're the guest borrowing my charger. Do you happen to be finished with it?"

I breathed out and moved to get the charger. My phone was at eighty percent, which was good enough. I unplugged everything and walked back to the door.

"Can you step back a bit?" I called through the thick wood.

He frowned but backed across the hall.

"A little further. Please."

His frown deepened, but he moved to the door of the room next to mine. I quickly opened my door, tossed out the charger, slammed the door shut, and locked it.

"Thank you!" I called. I watched as he walked over to pick up the charger, shaking his head the whole time. Not until I heard his heavy footsteps on the stairs did I move from the door to the bed.

Grabbing my phone to check the messages, I also readied the toothbrush to scrub my teeth clean. Moving the brush around my mouth, I swiped open my phone.

I ignored the messages from my friends. I couldn't handle those yet. Both my dad and Alec were checking in and wanted to hear from me right away. Especially Dad.

[Dad: Where are you?]

[Dad: Cailean McKay, answer me right now!]

[Alec: Hey, Dad is freaking out. Can you answer him? We just want to know you're safe.]

I put the toothbrush down, suddenly overwhelmed. Tears slid down my face, and I just sobbed. All my fear, anxiety, and pain poured out of me, and I let it flow—the hate, the relief, and everything in between. I was far from safe while hiding in the UK, but for tonight, I was free from torture and whatever nefarious plans Trip had in store for me. Tomorrow, I'd head to Bridget. I needed my family now more than ever.

No texts were answered that night, and I cried myself to sleep.

Chapter 8

The next morning, I felt worn out. I still jumped at every noise, so sleeping sucked. I often awoke sitting up in bed, gasping for air.

My phone was charged enough, and I wanted to get out of this country yesterday, so I didn't waste time getting ready. I brushed my teeth for six minutes, enjoying the clean feeling. I left my captive clothes in the garbage in the room, dropped the now-cold pasta on the desk, then slipped a soda bottle from the restaurant into one of the cargo pockets. I regretted putting my own sneakers back on, but I had no other options.

I ordered a taxi to the station using the concierge desk phone and waited inside the front door for it, surveilling the area. In this rain, everything felt dark and shadowy. Anyone could be hiding in plain sight. When the car pulled up, I rushed into the back seat and closed the door before repeating the process to double-check. I couldn't walk to Switzerland, so I had to risk being kidnapped again. The door was my best chance to escape if something happened, so I needed to know it would be unlocked for a quick exit.

"Sorry, I didn't think I closed it properly," I lied. "Can you take me to the York train station?"

"Not a problem." The driver drove off the hostel property without a second glance. I sat back and peered out the window, checking to see if we were being followed. After we pulled onto the highway and the rain fell harder, I had nothing else to do but watch the drops fall. Though the sky was a murky gray, the grass and gardens were happy, practically glowing bright green.

I thanked Brighde the driver knew I couldn't hold a conversation. If I spoke, I couldn't promise I wouldn't scream from my nerves being strung so tightly. My healing still wasn't completely back, and the problem was creeping its way into being my biggest one. I was lucky to manage closing the sores and blisters on my feet in the car, but nothing else would listen. At least I'd be able to walk without wincing.

The drive wasn't long, but with a building sense of urgency to head to Bridget, I counted the seconds until we arrived at the station. To distract myself, I bought a train ticket online. The feeling of having things prepared helped calm the growing anxiety. I wanted to cut down on any further delays.

"Thank you," I said, launching myself out the car.

"Thank you!" she replied as I closed the door. I barely registered when she drove away, as I was busy dashing into the station under the huge archway to locate my platform. Rushing down the stairs under the large hanging clock, I made it just as the train pulled in. Joining the morning rush, I followed a man in a business suit up the stairs, and as I looked for an available seat, the person behind me brushed their hands against my back. I flinched and knocked into the man in front of me. He turned around and glared at me.

"I'm sorry, I-I was bumped," I stammered. He nodded and faced forward again.

The guy found a seat, and I hurried past him, avoiding eye contact. Sliding in to claim an empty spot by the window in the back of the car, I felt grateful to have settled for now. According to Google, this trip would take me at least twelve and a half hours with several changes between trains and buses. As the train pulled out of the station toward King's Cross, I wished I could have hopped on a plane, but I was afraid Trip could track me easier if I flew. Plus, if he sent someone on the plane, I'd be trapped. A chill ran down my spine, and my wrists ached. I couldn't let that happen again.

For the two or so hours it took to get to King's Cross, the train was quiet. The only people who stopped by were conductors looking for my ticket. Everyone else kept moving, but I watched them until they left the car. I smelled coffee from somewhere, and I dully registered the need to eat something. Normally, I'd have toast with my breakfast, but I'd avoid bread for a while. Maybe I'd grab a granola bar when we got to the next station.

We pulled onto the platform, and the brakes squeaked their high-pitched song. I waited until my car was nearly empty of people before I got off, looking to see if anyone was watching me. I still didn't see anyone, so I calmly walked from the station, heading to St. Pancras International. My legs protested walking after the journey yesterday, but I ignored them and pushed on. I could rest soon.

St. Pancras was really a work of art. There were long lines of shops on the first floor, all brightly lit and welcoming. I found a newsstand with some snacks and a cooler. I purchased a drink and two granola bars, then walked upstairs to my train platform. The train wouldn't arrive for another thirty minutes, so I found a spot on the floor against a wall. I had the perfect vantage point to watch everyone and anyone who walked by. A family of tourists rushed past me. They were German, from the look of their suitcases and sound of their accents. Their little girl had pigtails and was trying to keep up with her dad, who held her hand tightly as he hurried by. It reminded me I hadn't answered Dad or Alec's texts from last night. But I didn't know what to say. Was I alright? Was I safe? I couldn't answer with honesty until I made it to the Academy.

I was so caught up in thought that I didn't see the train pull up. I hurried on just before the doors closed, and I walked through train cars before I found an empty seat next to someone. It was an aisle spot, which was fine for me, as my seatmate was ignoring me.

It was three and a half hours until we made it to our next stop. I was already so weary, but I didn't dare close my eyes. I wouldn't give anyone any opportunities. Maybe in Paris, I could crash for a while before I had to leave again. But if I felt the same way there as I did right now, I couldn't imagine that happening.

Thankfully, Eurostar was nothing eventful, and I was able to relax a little. Even when my neighbor fell asleep and slumped over, bumping his leg against mine, I didn't freak out like I had expected to. The warmth was nice, though the intrusion was unwelcome.

We arrived around eleven thirty in the morning. I was barely halfway to Switzerland, and I was exhausted, so I ate a granola bar, had a sip of my soda, and kept moving. My next train was leaving in thirty minutes from Gare de l'Est, and it was at least a ten-minute walk. It took all my might not to run from the stations. A tingling suspicion walked up my neck, and I spun around to see who was behind me. There was no one I recognized or who looked at me twice. One guy bumped into me as he walked past, so I followed him for a minute just in case. He didn't leave the station but headed to another track. *He's not here for you, Cay. You're safe for now. Keep going.*

Keeping my head down and weaving through throngs of tourists, children, businesspeople, and shoppers, I made it safely to the station with minutes to spare before the train arrived. I wasn't fully ready for food, but the sugar in the soda helped for now, so I took another sip. Out of the corner of my eye, I noticed a guy around my age waiting for our train on the same platform, but something about him put me on high alert. Black hair, tanned skin, long pants, an orange shirt, and a blue jacket. I didn't think he'd been on my previous trains, but my pulse raced, and I started to sweat as warning bells went off in my head. I watched him more intently than would be considered normal, but fear was growing in my stomach, and I couldn't take any chances. I had to make it to Switzerland.

When the train arrived, I watched as he got on a car in the back. I didn't want to get in the same car, but ignoring my gut, I moved to sit a few rows behind him. For the entire ride, he sat in his aisle seat, never once looking back. When we arrived in Strasbourg, I didn't move, but he left the train. I followed along as he disappeared into the crowd away from the platforms. With the potential crisis averted, I unclenched my jaw and took another sip of soda. It was warm and flat now, but I didn't mind. The train left ten minutes later, and then we were headed to Basel, Switzerland, where I would be one step closer to safety.

Somehow, I was able to sleep on the train, though I didn't feel tired. When we pulled into the station, I remained in my spot and stood to stretch. I wasn't as tall as Logan, but I got sore easily when confined to small spaces for long periods of time. Sitting back down, I eyed all the people who came into my car and sat. Anyone could have been a threat.

It felt like forever before we left the station, but we did, heading to our next stop in Switzerland: Spiez.

My stomach perked up at the scent of someone's sandwich, and I realized I had nothing else to eat but a granola bar I no longer wanted. Checking my phone, it was another three hours to Adelboden. I'd have to grab a snack or two from a cart, assuming anyone was still open. Drinking the last of my soda, I watched as houses, buildings, and trees passed us as we raced to the next stop.

That suspicion teased the back of my neck again, so I sat up straight and hunted for the person who caused it. This time, I'd fight back.

Most people were looking out the windows, reading on their phones, or seemingly sleeping. For a moment, I thought I saw the black-haired guy again, but even after blinking, I couldn't be sure if it was him. Sitting back, I had no blatantly obvious suspects, but that didn't mean someone wasn't lurking behind me, following my every move.

I stayed on the train again until we reached Frutigen. When it stopped and the doors opened, I ran to the next platform where the buses were located. There was a bathroom, which I stopped to use, and a vendor who was open until nine. I needed to keep something in my stomach, so I grabbed some chips and a candy bar, some kind of sandwich, and another soda. Out of the haul, I'd find something appeasing. I made it onto the bus just as the doors closed, then headed toward an open seat. I found an emptier section and sat for the half-hour journey. Snacking on chips helped the anxiety as I drew closer to Bridget. I would have to stop in Adelboden to ask for directions, but I expected to be there before the sunset.

Just to see if it'd work, I sent some healing waves to my body, boosting its energy level. My health bar would definitely be in the orange range if I were in a video game.

My stomach protested less than it had yesterday as I finished the chips and opened the soda, so I unwrapped the sandwich and took a bite. It was some bacon, cheese, turkey thing, but it was satisfying. It was nothing to write to Alec about—he and I loved finding interesting foods together.

I looked down, knowing I still hadn't replied to any messages. My throat tightened, and swallowing became difficult. It was too hard for me to tell them what was going on, but I also didn't want to lie to them. It was easier to deal with the guilt of remaining silent.

No longer interested in eating, I wrapped the sandwich and put it back into the bag from the vendor.

We arrived in Adelboden, and I breathed a sigh of relief. I was finally in the town where my best friends and family were located. Even my cuts were feeling better with the nearing hope I'd finally be safe again.

I walked out of the bus station and took in the scene in front of me. Brown-and-white buildings stood against a mountainous backdrop. Sharp points at the tops of houses and hotels with scalloped trim made me feel like I was in one of Grimm's fairy tales. I gave myself a minute to appreciate where I was before I scurried away to see who could point me toward Bridget.

Shops were closed, and I walked past darkened doorsteps. The only place that appeared open was a hotel, so I went in and headed to the front desk.

"*Grüessech,*" the clerk behind the desk said to me as I walked over.

"Um, hello," I replied meekly. *Stop it, you're safe! He is only here to help!* my internal voice berated me.

"Do you speak English?" I asked, firmer this time.

"*Ja,* I do. How can I help you?" he asked cheerfully.

"Um... Are there any schools or businesses, like... like a boarding school, here in Adelboden?" I crossed my fingers that he would understand what I was asking because I didn't know how else to ask without revealing everything. I got shit for pushing

Bridget into her destiny, but I didn't run around spilling everyone's secrets.

"Oh, *ja*, there is one just on the other side of the town, on your way to the Choleren Gorge." He gestured to the right of himself, which I assumed was the direction of the gorge.

"Thank you. Is there a quick way of getting there?"

The clerk looked at me, seemingly confused, before his face lit up. "*Ja*, keep walking down this road, and when it splits, go to the right. You won't miss it. It is the only structure in the area."

"*Danke*," I said, smiling. With that, I headed in the direction he told me to go.

The sun was beginning its descent as I trotted down the lane. The town was quiet except for my footsteps and the breath leaving my lungs. With every heartbeat, I was getting closer to Bridget and to feeling safe again.

A metallic skittering came from behind me, and I whipped around just as someone swung at me. I was knocked upside the head but not knocked down completely. Reeling, I turned and ran from the hotel toward my destination. I didn't get far, as my attacker grabbed the back of my shirt and yanked me back.

This can't happen again! Panic tore through me as I fell back onto the ground, the wind knocked out of me. I looked up in time to see a boot coming toward me, and I rolled into the street. By the luck of some Goddess, no cars were on the road, though I would take more interventional help right about now.

I got up and stood, facing my enemy. It was the black-haired guy from earlier today. He flashed a tattoo on the inside of his forearm—a completed

Amulet. Now Beira's descendants were *branding* themselves?

I shook my head to stop my mind from wandering. I put my hands up and gulped. I was in no shape to fight, especially since my healing had been failing me. My wrists protested their bent position, and my feet were sore, but I couldn't do anything aside from ignoring the pain. Otherwise, things were going to get a whole lot worse.

The descendant rushed me and grabbed my shirt, holding me up. I threw up my arms and blocked as many punches to the face as I could before he switched tactics. Once he let me go, I didn't react in time to deflect him from shoving his fist into my side repeatedly. I grunted in pain and kicked him right above the knee. He went down, and I turned and bolted, not wanting him to find Bridget. I ran past shops, my feet thudding against the ground. The sun was about to set, so I let darkness be my friend. Ducking between buildings, I ran down alleys that dumped me out behind the rows of shops, then paused, unsure of which way to go. *Pick any direction!* Darting to my right, I swerved around dumpsters and knocked over garbage, doing anything to slow him down. But all the noise would be leading him right to me.

Fuck.

I ducked behind a parked car next to some bushes. I pressed into them, hoping they would hide me. All was silent except for my panting, so I clapped my hand over my mouth.

In the quiet, I heard metal scraping metal, like a rod against dumpsters. I was prey, sitting open and vulnerable, ready to be eaten. It took everything inside me not to whimper. I was tired, and I was scared, but most of all, I was *not* going back to that fucking barn.

I climbed out of my hiding space and came face-to-face with him again.

"Do you have a name?" I asked, frustrated, scared, and tired. "I'd like to know who is planning on killing me. I'll go first. I'm Cay."

"I'm not going to kill you," he said, ignoring my request for his name.

"No?"

"No." He took a step forward, and I took one back. "Why not?"

He took another step forward, but I didn't move. "Those aren't my orders."

"So, what are they?" I was hoping if he kept talking, he would inflict less damage to my body.

But before I could blink, he launched himself at me.

"To send a message to the Cuardaitheoir."

Chapter 9

I didn't scream like I'd wanted to; instead, I accepted the attacker's body thrown against mine as I landed on my back again. I tucked my legs underneath him and pushed him off me, interrupting his trajectory. He nimbly fell, rolling to his side and popping up like a jack-in-the-box. I hopped up too, but I wasn't as graceful, giving him full access to kick me in the face. I turned my head, but not in time to avoid it or the feeling of my bones cracking as I stumbled backward. Blood gushed from my nose, and I wiped it with the back of my hand, not hopeful it would stop any time soon.

"Thanks for this," I said sarcastically, waving my bloody hand between us. "Can we consider this over?"

"Not yet," he replied, coming for me again. This time, I didn't care, and I ran again. Fighting was Alec's thing, not mine, and I'd had my fill of it. I dashed down another alley, this guy hot on my heels, so I leaped over a concrete stanchion like a gazelle. Landing hard on both feet, I grounded and kept running back toward the bus station. I made it past the hotel, then stopped and asked for directions before the descendant caught up and tackled me to the ground. To avoid facial damage, I craned my neck and pulled a muscle doing so. My palms were scratched and bleeding, rubble embedded into the skin. Bruises were blossoming on my arms and legs, nicely matching the cuts I already had.

The asshole grabbed my hair and yanked my head back.

"What's the message?" I asked, straining my voice.

He had the audacity to laugh. With that, he dropped my head and got off me. He kicked me countless times in the ribs and stomach. I groaned as pain ricocheted throughout my chest and down my legs. Curling up, I coughed, using the bit of energy I had left to expel the air.

I had no healing left in me. I was going to die.

Suddenly, he stopped, and I lay there, on the ground, wheezing and coughing.

"This isn't over," he said. Then he turned and ran down the hill that led to Adelboden.

"I seriously hope it fucking is," I muttered out loud.

Rolling over onto my back, I gagged at the blood dripping down my face. Bile rose in my throat, making me sit up and vomit. Blood and whatever food I'd eaten earlier made a reappearance in a way I didn't want to see.

My body spasmed as I threw up more. I didn't know how I had more to give. Vomiting after getting your ass kicked *sucked*.

When I was done, I crawled away from the mess to a sidewalk along the park. It was completely dark by now, and I knew I needed to get to Bridget before I was attacked *again*.

Putting one foot under me to push up, I collapsed, unable to support my weight. Panting, I tried again but fell, so I gave up. Crawling was the only mode of transportation that worked for me, so I relived my younger years and scooted as much as I could. I crawled my way down the street toward the school, leaving a trail of blood in my wake.

I couldn't say I made it very far, but I did go half a block before I gave up. When I finished, my body sung with agony, and I wanted to sleep. There was a garden up ahead that looked lush and soft, and most importantly, like a good place to rest. My wrists were bleeding again, and I didn't know if I cared anymore. I couldn't worry about them when the rest of me was failing at surviving. I knew my body was shutting down, and I didn't know how to stop it anymore. In a last-ditch effort, I sent any remaining healing to my body. A majority of it went to my nose, mending the broken bones, but only a few cuts were able to close partially, or least stop bleeding. Even with only one bruise gone, I'd take any bit of repair I could get. Stopping any ounce of the pain was worth it.

I gasped at the pain, trying to send some healing to my injuries, but nothing worked. I groaned and whimpered as my stomach clenched. Then I rolled over, vomiting nothing into the grass. The contractions were enough to make me want to scream. Lying back, I took shallow breaths through the pain. I stared at the stars above me and counted them in time with my breathing, keeping a slow tempo. It was like counting sheep, and my eyelids drooped. I tried to force them open because I didn't want to miss the stars shining, but I lost that fight. It was another one I couldn't win.

Again? Or was it the first time?

My eyes fluttered closed for a second, then popped back open, and I blinked to try and shake off the sleepiness. I was going somewhere. Where was I? I rolled my head over. I was lying on the side of the road in a patch of grass. Moving only my eyes, I looked at the brown-and-white buildings, which reminded me of something familiar I couldn't exactly remember. I sat up slowly to take in my surroundings. One of the buildings had a flag—red with a white cross in the center. What country had that emblem on their flag?

I swallowed firmly, familiar nausea creeping its way back in. To keep from throwing up, I breathed in through my nose and out through my mouth. My brain felt buzzy and chaotic, and I was *hot,* which was the perfect combination needed to vomit. Leaning over, I gagged, but nothing came out. Panting, I saw my dirty hands, covered in dried blood and with rocks pressed into the flesh. There were cuts and scrapes up my arms, and my legs looked worse. I sat up again and winced as I grabbed my stomach. Lifting the borrowed shirt, I saw a dark, purple bruise flourishing under my rib cage.

I needed help and healing but not in that order. As I tried and failed my healing once again, the injuries mocked me. *Who else could heal me?*

Bridget! Pushing myself up again, I started to crawl, focusing on making it past just one more storefront, one more block. This road felt shorter than when I'd been walking it before. Had it grown since then? The world spun and tilted slightly.

Closing my eyes, I willed the pain to go away. It was utterly unbearable. The pounding pulsated behind my eyes, and I wished for death to end it. Maybe I was dying. If this was how I went, I'd be pissed.

I kept going, pausing when needed, which was a lot. No one ever came to my rescue or saw me and tried to help. The road was empty and silent, the only noise coming from me as I held onto a bench and pulled myself up to a standing position. Alarm bells rang in my sore head, and I winced, pressing my palm to my skull. Once they subsided, I took a tentative step forward. Then another. I held onto garbage cans and streetlamps to keep going, but I needed to make it to Bridget. I didn't care if it would take me all night; I'd make it to the school.

I didn't know how far I'd gone, but somewhere in my stumbling, I had collapsed again because I woke up on the same road. Or it looked the same as the one before, so I couldn't be sure I was in the right place. Standing felt like too much effort, so the best option currently was crawling. My knees were torn up, red and angry, but I had no choice. My healing was broken, and I needed someone to fix me. I didn't know where the hospital was or if they could keep me safe. Bridget was my best hope, and with her was Logan, who would back me up in anything.

I made it farther, passing one shop at a time. The moon was high in the sky, so I relied on the lamps to guide me to the outskirts of town. Exhaustion weighed heavily on my bones and muscles, and pushing past it felt insurmountable. *What if I took a little nap here?* I stopped to look around me. It was concrete sidewalks, roads, and pathways around me. After a few more buildings, I saw pitch blackness.

My pulse quickened—what was waiting for me out there? Or who?

I had to get to Bridget, and this was the only way to get there. But what else would be out there waiting to kill me? Weighing my options spiked adrenaline in me, and I was able to stand and stumble forward. I didn't get very far, but any step closer was better than being where I was. I wished it were yesterday when I'd been sitting on a train in comfort. Or had that been the day before? I couldn't remember, flaring panic.

What if no one knew where I was? Who would find me? Unfortunately, Trip knew I was here. So at least one person would find me. Unless he left me here like he had in the barn. Flashes of being starved and chained came up, and I forced the images away. That was behind me, and right now, I needed to make it to the field. I'd been through enough.

Step by step, I made it forward until my foot hit the wispy grass of a field. I could no longer rely on the town lights to see. I gently patted my clothes, but my phone was gone, probably lost in the fight. Or the grass. I couldn't be sure.

Taking a deep, fortifying breath, I stepped into the darkness and let it embrace me.

A leg cramp hit, and I went down again, writhing in agony. Unsure what part of my body was killing me more, I breathed through the worst of it as my brain registered having landed on a rock. The humor was not lost on me, but I was in too much pain to muster a laugh.

As the cramp faded, I pulled myself up and continued down the path. The exhaustion was back, and I really needed a painless and restful break.

Dear Brighde, please don't let me be killed or run into a snake.

I left the path for about twenty paces and lay down in it. It was cool out but not uncomfortable. My sense of urgency to get to Bridget was diminished, and I was able to relax. As my muscles eased, I coughed and winced but was able to control my breathing and the pain, allowing me to fall asleep.

I woke sometime later as the sun was peeking over the horizon. It was cooler now, and I was shivering, which set off all the pain from before. At least the dull thud in my head was less violent than it had been. Something soft rubbed against me, and I looked to see a baby deer sniffing me. I froze. The last thing I wanted was a disease or another injury, but at this rate, I was collecting both like Pokémon. It licked my leg and then jumped over me. It scared the shit out of me, and I tucked my body up into a ball.

While I waited for darkness to take me over, I looked around at what my last memory would be. The field was beautiful, dotted with purple and white flowers. The grass wasn't the same bright green as we had at home, but it was similar to prairie grass, soft and yellowish green. In the distance, I saw a square, and the shape came into focus as I squinted. It looked like a large hotel, similar to the one by the bus depot. I hoped to Brighde this was the school.

Feeling inspired, I dragged myself up and started the trek to Bridget. I ignored the pain that radiated throughout my body with every footstep and didn't break, no matter how much my body demanded it. It took me longer than I thought because things were a bit blurry—I wasn't sure I was seeing the pathway clearly anymore. Blinking and rubbing my eyes didn't help. The sun had just finished waking up, so I had no time to waste. Right now, I was too exposed to the elements and further attacks.

As I came up on the front walk of the school, the building loomed above me. Dirty, red doors were surrounded by the same dark-brown wood that every other building had, but there were no scalloped edges or charming tulips. Nothing was inviting. Ignoring my gut reaction to run, I hobbled to the front door and pushed. It creaked open, the sound bouncing off the walls inside. I closed it behind me, letting my eyes adjust to the dimness in the room. There was a staircase in front of me with a large window on the top landing, which provided a lot of light in the room. I peeked around, waiting to see if anyone would come to greet me. While I waited, my bladder remembered it needed release. Stumbling around and looking into closed doors, I found a dining room, offices, and a library, but no bathroom. Heading back to the main hall, I gazed at the stairs, dreading the climb. The light coming in from the window was blinding, and I held my hand up to block the sun. If my bladder wasn't urging me on, I would have said, "Fuck it," and lay right there on the floor. But taking the stairs one at a time, I climbed to the first entry. I didn't know what this floor was, but I hoped there would be a toilet.

Opening the door as silently as I could, I toddled down the hall, leaning against the wall for support. Doors were on every side, and I saw some artwork or notes tacked on the panels. I guessed these were dorm rooms, and hopefully one was keeping Bridget safe and sound. First, I'd hit the bathroom, and then I'd find my cousin.

Thankfully, the bathroom was in the center of the hallway, and I went inside, not caring what the sign said. No one seemed to be up yet, so I had the large lavatory with urinals to myself.

I finished, zipped my shorts, and went to the sink to clean up. Finally seeing my face in the mirror, I noticed I needed serious repair. Cuts and bruises laced my face, and dried blood and bile were smeared around my mouth and nose. I grabbed a paper towel and wet it, trying to wash off the worst of it all. Everything was tender to the touch, and washing my hands was detrimental as I tore open one of the gashes, causing it to bleed again. Using another paper towel, I applied pressure to slow it down. When I pulled the towel away, the opening looked more secure. After cleaning my blood off the sink and my body as much as I could, I threw the towels into the trash and opened the door in hopes of finding Bridget.

After the strenuous activity, I didn't make it very far, collapsing in a heap in the hall. My legs gave out, and the thudding in my head had grown. A door down the hall opened, and a figure walked out. Squinting, I tried to make them out, but it wasn't until they came toward me that I realized who it was.

"Bridget, where the hell were you?" I asked when I recognized her, trying to lift my head up. It was too hard and required so much effort, so I left it on the ground.

"Cay! Cay? I'm here. I didn't go anywhere." She cradled my head, and immediate relief flooded my system. Like just being around her, I could start to truly heal.

"I couldn't find you," I told her softly, allowing my body to crash. I was so tired, and now that I was with my family, I could sleep without worry.

"What you mean?" she asked, smoothing my hair away from my face. It was such a motherly movement that I nearly cried.

"I searched for you. When I escaped." My eyelids drooped and blocked out the light as I sighed. "I knew you could save me," I whispered, hoping she heard me.

I was safe. I'd found her.

Pronunciation

Cuardaitheoir (koor-DA-hoir)	Seeker
Brighde (Breed)	A Scottish goddess who, with the help of an Amulet, was able to control the Summer seasons (Spring and Summer)
Beira (Beer-a):	A Scottish goddess who, with the help of an Amulet, was able to control the Winter seasons (Fall and Winter)
Neit (Neat)	Scottish God of War; the name of Cailean's dog
Cailean (Kay-lin)	
Sfera con Sfera (s-fera con s-fera)	A sphere within a sphere—an art exhibit installed in locales around the world, including Dublin.

About The Authors

Both Leslie and Janice Sommers were raised in New Jersey but have a little New York sass to them (courtesy of Janice's hometown of Bay Ridge, Brooklyn). This duo is known in their respective friend circles as the "funny one" and often is sought out to make others laugh. Janice has always been found with a book in her hands and spent most of Leslie's childhood reading to her children. Reading and writing YA Fantasy have always come naturally to Leslie, getting this from her mother, so it was a no-brainer for them to co-write a series. If reading is their hobby, then writing is their passion. Teaching herself to read and create stories at 3 years old, Leslie knew this was what she wanted to do. Though the Amulet series is their first, they have already been working on a second series, steeped in fantasy and romance. You can follow them on Twitter and Instagram at lj_sommers and TikTok as lj_sommers_author, and Leslie can be found on Facebook as Leslie Sommers. If you're lucky, you can catch them in the wild stacks of their local library, working through the new YA fantasies (and some contemporary romances) that were just released or assembling non-official book clubs with new friends.

Book Club Questions

1. Who do you think let Cay go free and why? Or do you think leaving the key was an accident?

2. Why do you think Trip has a sudden change of heart and tries to help Cay?

3. Do you think Cay would have been kidnapped if he had stayed with Logan? Why or why not?

4. Cay keeps asking Bridget if keeping the Amulet around her neck is the safest place for it. What do you think and why?

5. Why do you think Cay's healing failed him after he was tortured? Explain.

Discover more at
4HorsemenPublications.com

10% off using HORSEMEN10